D0648464

KING

Books by Lonnie Coleman

NOVELS

Escape the Thunder

Time Moving West

The Sound of Spanish Voices

Clara

Adams' Way

The Southern Lady

Sam

The Golden Vanity

King

SHORT STORIES

Ship's Company

PLAYS

Next of Kin

Jolly's Progress

A Warm Body

McGraw-Hill Book Company

NEW YORK TORONTO LONDON SYDNEY

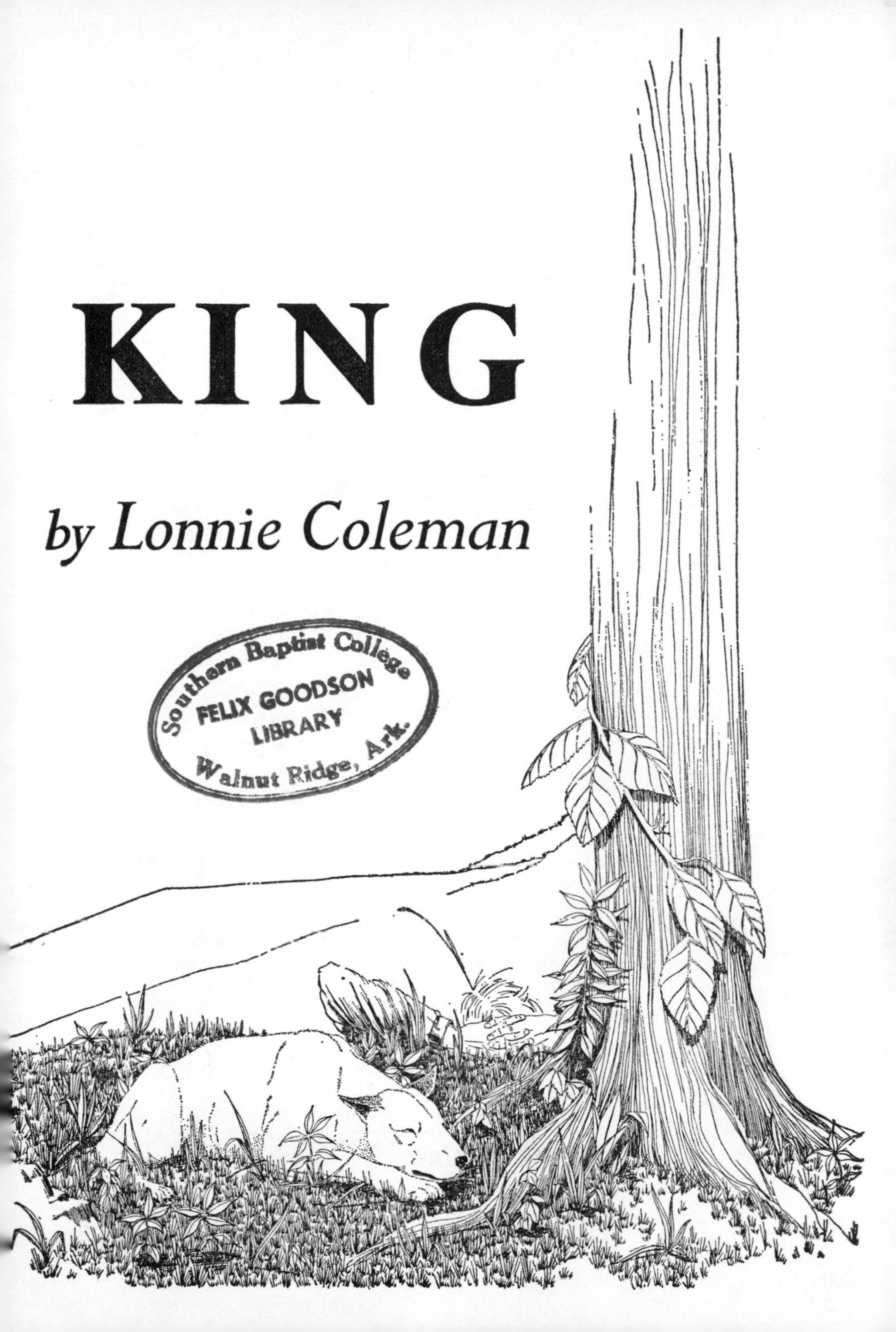

KING

by Lonnie Coleman

KING

Printed in the United States of America.

Library of Congress Catalog Card Number: 67-24435

Second Printing 11785

To the happy
and loving memory of
NICHOLAS WREDEN

KING

Chapter

1

I DID MUCH of my growing up in a little town in Central Georgia in the twenties. The population of the town then was about five hundred. Now it's less. Those country towns, once shopping, banking, and cotton-ginning centers for surrounding farms, were killed by the Depression and the automobile and the decline in the importance of cotton as a money crop. But at the time I tell of the town I lived in was Eden for a boy.

The roads were not yet paved. In summer, when the heat shimmered in the air and rain had been scarce, the dirt roads were powder, and my bare footsteps raised clouds as I walked. The passing of a car sent me choking and running to jump the ditch to the hard-packed dirt sidewalk, like pavement itself, and just as hot to my bare feet. The tufts of grass along the sides and edges which kept the sidewalk from eroding were oases for burning feet. When it rained, to walk was to wade through mud. Spatters of mud streaked my legs up to the thigh where my khaki shorts or rolled-up overalls began. To squeeze the mud between my toes was a delicious experiment in depravity.

In winter the earth was often frozen, with ice in the ditch and anywhere a puddle of water had been yesterday. The ruts of car and wagon wheels were hard and sculptural.

The only real paved sidewalk was in the couple of blocks of the business center across from the train depot. There were the two banks, the post office, a barbershop, a drugstore, and three general stores where the smell of a thousand things became one smell, however various a compound of nails, bolts of cloth, groceries, candy (my favorites were the chocolates shaped and wrapped to look like small silver bells), coffins, harness, vinegar, kerosene, and new shoes. This was the part of town everyone meant when they said they were "going to town." There were two trains a day, the Up Train at eleven in the morning, and the Down Train at three in the afternoon. There were sometimes special trains early in the morning that carried us to Savannah on excursion rates. People generally, at least one member of a family, managed to be in town around traintime. The women and the young people frequented the drugstore; the men hung around the banks or the barbershop, waiting for mail to be sorted.

Across the tracks and beyond the depot were modest houses, set not very close together, becoming grander but never very grand as the churches were passed and "the hill" lay ahead. The churches were two, Baptist and Methodist, set in the same shady grove of trees. Sitting in one church we could sometimes hear the tone of sermon or song in the other. There was rivalry between the churches, but never bad feeling. The Baptists looked down on the Methodists, and the Methodists looked down on the Baptists, but everyone was friendly and polite about it. A joke enjoyed by all was that when one congregation sang "Will There Be Any Stars in My Crown?" the answering hymn of the other was "No, Not One."

People from nearby farms left their cars and buggies in the grove while they enjoyed spiritual instruction inside. And enjoy it they did, at least the adults. The women sat still and attentive with patient looks on their faces, making an occasional slight shift of position on the hard pews slowly, with dignity, so that no rustle of apparel intruded on the religious atmosphere. Only in summer was the scene livelier. The windows were open, diluting the musty, sanctified air with a fresher smell, and the rhythmic movement of the cardboard fans of the women made a sound like birds on the wing. The occasional dropping of a fan to the floor and the retrieving of it were done with a self-admonishing smile.

The men sat stiffly, seeming to pride themselves on how long they could sit without moving or blinking. Even the children were fairly still. *They had better be,* said the flash in a mother's eyes at the restless squirming of a cub. The father ignored them. Light discipline was the job of the mother. If that failed, the child knew that later, at home, he would have to face Father with the belt or strap.

In the main, though, people enjoyed church. Even my uncle, who was not much of a churchgoer, was heard to say on the two or three occasions a year he did attend that he enjoyed a really *good* sermon. The implication was that the preacher made a special effort when he saw Uncle there and that his lesser efforts served very well for the rest of us the rest of the time.

One thing about church was that you saw almost everybody you knew all together. After Sunday school and the sermon the children were allowed to run and play in the grove, the town children getting to know the country children, inventing secrets and scandals, beginning loves and grudges that sometimes were to last a lifetime. The women chatted with the women on the porch and steps of the churches, and the men talked to the men below the steps in the churchyard about crops and politics and conditions.

When Uncle came to church Aunt always, before leaving for home and midday dinner, led Uncle and me across the road to the cemetery shared by both congregations. There she would stand, looking intently at the grave and headstone of her only child, a girl who had died at four. Uncle and I waited mutely. After a bit Aunt would blink her eyes, hold her handkerchief briefly to her nose, square her shoulders, and turn to us with a smile.

We lived in the other direction, away from the main residential section. Back past the depot and the "town" were the icehouse and the filling station that was soon to make obsolete the blacksmith shop which stood next to it. The loyalty of the town boys was about to shift to the filling station, but when I first went to live there, the blacksmith shop still held us. We would stand or squat in a loose ring watching the smith work. He noticed us seldom as he pounded and bent white-hot, red-hot metal into wondrous shapes, but once in a while, if he were not overbusy, he'd make rings for us out of horseshoe nails. We wore them

"That's my sister Johnny-May," Lamar explained. "She cusses. I don't know where she gets it. Not from me and not from Mama. Tie your sash, Johnny-May, and keep your dress down. It don't look nice showing your tail thataway." She gave her dress a yank. "Come on," he said to me.

"Why don't my flowers grow?" she demanded of us, but we neither turned nor answered.

Johnny-May was forever digging up ferns and flowers in the woods, then sticking them in a hole in her garden, as she called it, only to have them die on her. It was only when Aunt took her in hand that she learned to grow things. Aunt could grow anything. She got Johnny-May over her cussing, too, finally. I imagine Aunt saw in Johnny-May something of her own little girl who died. Johnny-May's mother couldn't do a thing with her; in fact, she was terrified of that child, although she was quick enough to give Lamar a slap if he did something she thought wrong.

Johnny-May doesn't have a big part in this story, so it won't hurt to tell how she turned out. Her cussing and hating bloomers and a stubborn streak a yard wide certainly didn't promise well, but I guess Aunt taught her gradually how to be a girl. By the time she had finished high school she was all right. She turned out pretty. The chalk-white hair she'd had when she was little darkened into a nice blond color, and her pudgy face thinned out into something that looked even refined. She went into nurses' training in Augusta and married a doctor. She and her husband Henry and four children live in Charleston now. I saw them when they came to New York for the World's Fair. We had dinner together, and while Henry was busy studying the menu with the children, I said to Johnny-May,

"Pull your dress down, Johnny-May." She looked at me blankly a second, then remembered and laughed. She laughed so hard Henry and the children looked up a question at us, but she didn't explain. For a minute there she was again that little girl I first saw, showing her bottom and calling the world shit-ass.

Lamar and Johnny-May lived alone with their mother. I found out that their father had run away to Florida with some woman from Wrens he met when he went over there to see a baseball game. He sent them a little money from time to time, but they never knew how much it would be or how long it would have to last, and they had it pretty hard. Aunt May took in sewing. She was especially in demand making wedding dresses for the colored people. They almost all came to her. She copied fashions from the latest Sears, Roebuck catalogue, but she added ideas of her own, Aunt said. The house always seemed full of pins and scraps of cloth, and Aunt May's bed which she shared with Johnny-May always seemed to be covered with a dress pattern cut out of newspaper.

It was knowing the Salters that showed me the position Uncle had. He was no rich man, but he owned several farms and a sawmill. Our house had electric lights and plumbing and real rugs on the floor. The Salters had a linoleum rug in their living room and no rugs anywhere else. They used kerosene lamps and they had an outhouse that hung over the creek. Naturally, I thought it preferable to our bathroom. Its builder—the owner before the Salters—had provided it with three holes, so that presumably three people could sit companionably side by side. There were two large holes and one small one. I was never there with anyone but Lamar, and we went only on serious business. Urinating was done by a boy wherever the urge caught him, so long as no one was around and there was something interesting to pee on. A man or a boy has to have something to pee on, I've noticed, even if it's just a rock or a wall.

So much of our life centered on the creek. The Salters lived right on it, and it was nothing to step into Lamar's boat and shove off and be gone. It seems to me we spent a million years floating or rowing or poling up and down that creek. It was a time out of time, the mossy cypresses over us, the funny, different calls of birds, the plop of a fish leaping out of water or a turtle dropping into it from a log.

Unlike his sister and mother, who were fair, Lamar was dark-skinned and had black curly hair, a regular mop of it. He was tall and skinny then with big eyes and big front teeth. All you saw at first was hair and eyes and teeth, and he often went with his mouth partly open, not foolishly, but thoughtfully.

Such were the town and our nearest neighbors when I, orphaned at seven by a car crash, went to live with Aunt and Uncle. Lamar was my best friend until he got nearly grown and worked at the filling station and started going out with girls. He was killed over Guadalcanal during the Second World War, but of course nobody could know then that's what would happen.

Chapter

2

In summer I was often up before Aunt and Uncle, and they were early risers. My room was at the back of the house, opening onto the porch. It took only a minute to slip into shorts or overalls. When it was warm, I wore no shirt unless I was going to town. In cool weather I added a shirt, sometimes a pull-over sweater, socks and shoes. The thing was to get out quickly; there was so much to see and do.

I had been a city boy, and in the city there was nothing for me to do when I woke but wait until others woke, or if I got up and dressed to be quiet about it and look at a book. The only outdoors for me had been the park, and that was nothing to this.

This was all mine: my fields, my woods, my creek, my town. I don't remember that any restriction was ever made on my movements. At first Aunt tried to keep me from climbing the windmill, but she soon gave that up, begging me only to hold on tight the higher I went.

I didn't forget my mother and father, but the violence and suddenness of their end were a death for me, too; coming here to live, another birth. I thought of my parents only when they were mentioned, usually by Aunt, and my tears when they came were not entirely honest. The business of the young is not to sorrow but to survive.

Out the door and into the yard! The chickens were long up and scratching near the house. Already they were used to me. Past the row of neat hen houses with their neat steps for the hens to walk up and down, a sight that always amused me because they looked so thoughtful about it. Then the pig yard. The foolish things, although they knew it was not I bringing their slops so early, always ran to the fence, jostling and grunting and squealing to be nearest their feeding trough. When I came back later in the morning to feed them with Uncle, or sometimes Aunt, I'd climb the fence and sit on its top rough board to watch them gobble up their slops. Watching animals eat is a pleasant, untaxing occupation.

My next visit was to the cowshed. Those quiet creatures with their solemn, unblinking eyes stared at me and mooed expectantly, wanting to give up their milk from veined, heavy bags, grown uncomfortable overnight. The barn cat waited at the gate of the cowshed for his warm morning milk which Aunt gave him in a bent blackened piepan. No one had bothered to name him anything but Tom, and his job was simply to keep the rats down in the barn. Aunt's house cat, Mildred, was a dainty creature who spent most of her time washing herself or following Aunt about the house to watch her at her various chores. Mildred was black and white, nicely marked. Tom was a tabby. They had nothing to do with each other except on those occasions that led to Mildred's pregnancies.

When everyone we could think of had been supplied with a kitten and no one would accept another, the offspring of Tom and Mildred were taken to the creek and drowned. I thought it a terrible thing and once contrived to free the kittens in the woods. Uncle explained to me that they would starve, or become the prey of stronger animals. He pointed to a hawk watching us from the low limb of a tree and told me what would happen when we left them. He said that if by chance the hardiest survived, it would grow up wild and prey for food on the birds I was beginning to know. It was a hard lesson, one I have never altogether learned: that of choice, selection, suppression of certain animal lives for the betterment of all.

I begged. I promised to look harder for homes for them. I offered to give my own food to them, just so they should live. But he shook his head, finally, impatiently. Trying not to cry, I gathered the blind kittens and kissed each one before putting it back into the sack. He softened toward me when I handed him the sack. Taking me by the shoulder, he turned me toward home while he continued with his live burden toward the creek.

Sometimes on my early-morning excursions I joined Lamar who had a routine of examining the lines he set out for fish. More often not. There were plenty of times to be with Lamar, and I think he preferred, as I did, to be alone in the morning. The discovery of the world needed no human companion.

There were tracks to be examined to ask Uncle about at breakfast. A night could make a difference in the budding of a tree in spring, the falling of its leaves in autumn. A night could change the shape of a sand bar, leave interesting, new refuse on its shore, shift however slightly the position of a log that lay half in, half out of water. The very air had its secrets of scent and sound to be pondered.

The first excursion of the day over, I hurried home to breakfast. I was not a boy who forgot about meals. I loved food and never needed urging to justify the breakfasts Aunt cooked. The kitchen was only one of her particular elements, but to see her there was to know her best. She was a small woman, just a little plump, and it was a pleasure to watch her quick, knowing movements, the brief speculation in her eyes before adding more salt or pepper to a dish.

Always there were eggs, fried or scrambled. Always there were hot biscuits, sometimes sweet-potato biscuits or crackling bread. The meat might be fried ham or sausages or pork chops. Sometimes rabbit or chicken simmered in thick crusty gravy. Grits always. Pancakes sometimes. Milk and coffee, syrup and jams, a wedge of pie or cake.

In winter we ate at a round table in the big kitchen; in summer at an oblong table on the screened-in back porch. There was a formal dining room, but it was used only when there were guests. Eating was a serious business, but never a solemn one. Even when his mind was occupied with business matters of the farms or the sawmill, Uncle relished a piece of gossip or speculation Aunt had picked up about the people we knew, and often he himself had a story to tell about the families who worked the farms or about the sawmill hands. We were, it seems to me, a family from the beginning. If they had to make room for me in their lives, they did it so naturally I never knew it.

One morning at breakfast Uncle announced that I was to have a dog. Furthermore, I could choose him and name him.

"Where? When?"

"Wait." He smiled and winked at Aunt.

Late in the afternoon, when he returned from his round of work in his Ford, Uncle brought with him a fat white bull terrier. She sat on the front seat beside him, regally, as if she were quite used to being driven about. Uncle was a tall lean man who moved with assurance and even deliberation but now he got out of the car quickly and held the door open for the fat creature to waddle out. She stopped and looked about, assessing me and her surroundings.

"Is that him?" I was disappointed.

Uncle's eyes narrowed with amusement, but he did not laugh. "No, that's her. Her name is Queenie."

"You said I was to choose—you said I was to name him!"

"So you shall." He called to Aunt and she came from the kitchen to the back door. "Have you got an old something to make her bed?"

Aunt nodded and disappeared.

"She just showed up by herself at the sawmill one day last week. The men took care of her and called her Queenie. You think it suits her?"

"I guess so."

"She's going to have puppies."

At last I understood. "How many?"

"I don't know."

"I can choose any one I want?"

"Any one."

"I want a boy dog."

"All right."

"How will I know which one?"

He smiled faintly, remembering perhaps the first time he'd made such a choice. "I think you'll know."

"How soon will she have them?"

"Can't say. Soon, though."

"Hurry up, Queenie, hurry up!"

"Whoa!" Laughing, he caught me around the waist and stopped me from shaking Queenie, who had taken the indignity from a stranger with remarkably easy temper. Aunt returned, carrying a worn, clean quilt, faded from many washings.

We made a procession to the barn: Aunt, Uncle, Queenie, and I. I found a box in the loft. Aunt lined it with the quilt. Queenie quietly took possession.

The following days Queenie was the center of my life. As soon as I was out of bed I went to her. She never wandered far from her box, and I was allowed to carry her food to her. The chickens and the cows and the pigs were unimportant now. Mildred and Tom went without their morning pat and cuddle. Every minute I was not in school I hovered over the fat, ugly dog. She tolerated my company, accepted the food I brought her, but she did not share my feeling of urgency about the important event to come. "Come on, Queenie, come on," I coaxed her, as if she were running last in a race.

"Will the puppies look like her?" I asked Aunt.

"Lord knows," Aunt said, and laughed.

I frowned. "I don't care if they do. I'll love mine anyway."

It happened one night after supper. I had paid my last regular visit of the day to Queenie earlier. It had been brief. I was disgusted with her for being so slow. Aunt had finished in the kitchen and settled down in the living room to her embroidery. She was working on a table scarf. It was already thick with flowers and bees and one butterfly, and she had begun to finish the stems of the flowers and the grass with dark green thread. I idly watched her for a bit before getting out a storybook. In the second grade we were not yet given much homework. After a while Uncle came in smiling. "She's started," he said to Aunt. She looked quickly at me.

I knew he meant Queenie. "Have they come?" I asked, thrilled.

"No. She was just starting when I left her."

"Is she all right?" Aunt asked.

He nodded. "I'm going back."

"Can I come?" I asked.

"No," Aunt said.

"Please, Aunt!"

"No." She bit off a thread.

"I think maybe he should," Uncle said quietly, after a look at me. I held my breath. They looked at each other. I waited.

"If you think so," Aunt said.

"Come on, boy."

I raced for the back door, found the lantern Uncle had left on the steps, and took it up. "Hurry, Uncle!"

"Wait!" he commanded. I stopped in my tracks. He took the lantern from me and with his other hand took one of mine. "You've never seen this before. I want you to be quiet. It's important. Queenie has a job to do, and she knows how to do it. All we can do is stay with her. No noise, you hear?"

"Yes, sir."

Together we marched to the barn and found the corner with Queenie's box. Uncle set the lantern down, close enough for us to see Queenie and for her to see us, but we kept back in the dark.

One of the pups had just been born. It was a different Queenie I saw from the one I had known. Gone was her benign indifference. She was busy cleaning the newly born even as the head of a second began to emerge. I watched with curiosity and awe. Uncle pressed my hand slightly and let it go. I did not move. I breathed as little and as shallowly as I could. I must have been frowning with concentration because after a while Uncle whispered, "Don't worry. She's doing fine."

Certainly Queenie was not worrying. She was efficiently busy. The second pup was out now and cleaned. Was that to be all? No. After a short wait the head of the third began to emerge.

I felt Uncle's hand on my shoulder. "Take it easy."

I barely heard him.

What made me know? "That's the one," I whispered hoarsely about the pup that was only half born. Uncle pressed my shoulder, whether from agreement or to admonish me to be quiet I didn't know. Then he was fully born. Queenie licked his face and head and back and belly and behind, and he was clean. When she turned him over with her nose and tongue I saw that he was a male.

"Wait," Uncle said.

A fourth pup had begun to show his head, but I was no longer interested in the repetition of birth. I knew everything, as Queenie did, and I had eyes and attention only for the one I had chosen. I had already memorized his markings. He was all white except for brown-tipped ears and a tail that was half brown beginning at its end. In the dark behind us there was a slight sound.

Aunt held out a tin piepan. "I thought she might be hungry after," she said. "I brought some clabber milk. I poured some syrup on it to sweeten it."

Uncle nodded and took the pan. Aunt left. We waited, but there were no more. The fourth pup was clean. All were wriggling to show a little life around Queenie's nipples. Presently Queenie looked at Uncle and gave a twitching wag of her bobbed tail. "Good dog," Uncle said and moved to her. I had never heard him speak so gently. He lowered his hand slowly to her head, let her sniff it, stroked her head once, approvingly. She looked quickly, with almost comical surprise, at her pups, then back at Uncle with pride. "Good dog," he said again, and laughed very low. He turned to me. "Come over, boy." My throat was tight as I joined him. But when he spoke again the whole atmosphere seemed to have lightened. He no longer whispered; his voice was teasing. "I bet you don't know which one you picked out."

"Yes, sir." I protested. "That one!" I pointed to mine.

"Well," he said.

Queenie got to her feet a little stiffly, one pup—mine—

the last to be shaken from her teats. When she found a solid balance, Uncle held the pan of clabber milk below her muzzle. She ate it all, quickly and greedily.

"Shouldn't she—shouldn't she be—?" I was anxious, my eyes on my pup.

"They're all right."

When Queenie finished eating she tidied her box and settled down again. The pups nuzzled close to her, and she looked down at them contentedly.

I reached out a hand.

"Better not yet."

I pulled my hand back.

"Let's leave her alone," Uncle said.

"Will they be all right?"

He took up the lantern, and I saw his nod in the light it gave. "You can see them first thing in the morning." He held the lantern close to Queenie's box so that we could have a last look. Without turning his face to me he said, his voice again lightly teasing, "Bet you won't remember in the morning which one."

"Yes, I will. That one."

He looked after my pointing finger.

"The third one born," I said.

"Oh. Have you decided on a name?"

"King."

He nodded, unsurprised.

We left the barn, walking a little stiff-legged after our vigil. We didn't talk. We were two men together, we had seen life begin. Afterward, I realized it was that night I began to love Uncle.

Chapter 3

AFTER THAT there was never enough time for everything. School became for me a long, boring, squirming pause between things that mattered, although before King I had liked school more than not. And then there was that hateful piano. In the living room Aunt had a victrola and a piano. The records were simple ones, but I never tired of playing them. The ones I remember best were "Little Brown Jug," "In a Little Spanish Town," and "Ramona." Neither Aunt nor Uncle played the piano. She had bought it hopefully for her little girl.

Soon after I went to live with them and was investigating everything in the house, I opened the keyboard of the piano and picked out that thing every child seems to know that goes acker backer soda cracker, acker backer boo. I don't remember where or how I learned it. Anyway, suddenly Aunt was standing there in the doorway drying her hands on her apron, having come from the kitchen. Thinking maybe she liked the tune I played it for her again and then a third time. Her eyes were alert with an idea when she nodded and left me. If I'd known what that idea was going to cost me in wasted time I'd have felt like cutting off my hands.

That night at supper she brought up with Uncle the proposition of my taking piano. There was, she said, a good teacher who taught right there in school. She had already been on the telephone to Miss Spiers at the boarding house where some of the teachers from out of town lived, and Miss Spiers had said why, yes, she could take me on for an hour after school two days a week from three to four o'clock, and if I promised in addition to practice an hour a day three other days a week at home by myself, *she'd* promise to have me in shape to play a little piece in the recital given in the spring near the end of the school year. I saw what I'd got myself into.

I took hope briefly when Uncle lowered his head and began hemming and hawing. "It'll keep him indoors a lot. Oughtn't he to be out as much as he can be?"

Aunt wouldn't listen. She might have been championing the cause of neglected genius. Franz Liszt would not hammer on the door of immortality in vain if she could help it. "You should have heard him today when he came home for dinner! He went to the piano and actually played a little piece he must have taught himself." Uncle had taken his midday meal at the sawmill and so missed my performance.

He looked at me. "What do you say, boy?"

I felt sick. I didn't know what to say. I wanted to please her, and I knew I couldn't go against that look in her eyes.

If I'd known what it would mean I'd have found the courage to oppose her, but I didn't know. "I never thought about it." A shrug. "I don't care."

So it was arranged. I took my lessons on Tuesday and Thursday afternoons and on Mondays, Wednesdays, and Fridays I had to go home right after school and practice. It was an awful thing that had happened. I started with indifference to music and soon developed a burning hatred for it. I think all of us knew pretty quickly that I had no talent—Uncle, Miss Spiers, even Aunt. All of Miss Spiers' patience and all of my application bore no fruit. I couldn't even play the simple scales without hitting wrong notes. It seemed to me preposterous that those black-and-white symbols on a sheet of music could have anything to do with the black-and-white keys of the piano, or that either could have anything to do with melody.

However, nobody except me was willing to give it up without a thorough try. I was even given what was to be my recital piece, a duncy, jiggling thing called "Over the Candy Counter." I must have played through it, or tried to, more times than there are hairs in the beard of the Prophet. Even today, so many years later, when I hear a certain combination of notes that reminds me of that piece, my mouth goes dry and my fingers numb.

So now when I had a dog I was denied his company for an extra hour every day, besides school. For, as he got older, the one thing King would not do for me was sit in the living room while I banged away at scales. It scared him, and no wonder.

But all was not ashes in the oatmeal. He *was* with me most of the time. The morning after he was born Lamar and Johnny-May came over to see the puppies, Johnny-May pronouncing them the cutest little shit-asses she'd ever seen. Her repertory of dirty words was not extensive, but she used those she knew with a will.

There were other visitors. It seemed to me the whole town came at one time or another to see Queenie and her brood. It couldn't have been so; still, many came. They were the only white bull terriers in town. The three other pups had been promised as soon as they were weaned, and the people who were to have them had to come and see how they were getting along and bring other people with them to show them off. Uncle had chosen to give the extra pups to people who worked his farms, because he knew I wanted mine to be the only one of his kind in town. Queenie was eventually returned to the sawmill where she became a sort of mascot and ratter. She left one day with Uncle looking as regal and unconcerned sitting on the seat beside him as she had the day he'd brought her. She stayed at the sawmill about a year and then just drifted off one night as mysteriously as she had appeared.

But that wasn't yet.

Curiously, I don't remember King as a puppy very well because I had him so long as a grown dog. I do remember that he was never gangly or clumsy. He seemed to me perfectly formed, a beautiful dog with intelligent eyes that could reflect every mood, mild or fierce—puzzlement, interest, content, anger, hurt, sorrow, mirth, boredom.

The brown markings on his ears and tail tips were soon lost—and that was the only time I had any use for that sorry piano of Aunt's. I had known in a general way that the ears and tails of the pups would be clipped; it was the custom then with such dogs. The word "clipped" sounded so neat and innocent I hadn't worried about it. One afternoon Uncle brought home with him the man to do the clipping. I didn't see him, didn't know what was about to happen. I was at the piano going through some scales.

Aunt usually went about her business while I practiced, but that day she came into the living room and settled down in a rocking chair. It was out of character for her to sit idle with no work in her lap, but my trouble with the scales had dulled my powers of observation. Presently I heard a horrible sound of Queenie's fierce, urgent, angry, outraged barking, and along with it, soprano to her alto, the frightened, shrill, hurting wails of the pups.

I flew from the piano bench toward the door, but Aunt caught me before I got there, caught me and held me. "It's all right—they're clipping them—be over in a minute—hurts just for a minute—they won't even remember—"

I struggled, but she held me until I crumpled against her. The racket outside had increased, the cows and the pigs and the chickens raising a sympathetic alarm. But I could still hear the dogs—*my* dog, I was sure.

Aunt pulled me over to the piano and sat me down on the bench. "Play!—Bang!—Make noise!" she urged, holding her hands over her ears. It was only then I knew that she suffered with the dogs, too. I pounded the keyboard of the piano in harsh discords as loud as I could make them. I pounded until I was exhausted, until we both realized the sound of the dogs had ceased. Aunt let me off the rest of that day's practice.

When I saw King, he was all right. That is to say he was himself, perfectly self-possessed, no scars other than the physical ones. It took them some time to heal, because he scratched or rubbed his scabs off and then had to live through new ones. By then Queenie had taken her departure and the rest of her brood had gone to their homes in the country. When, on occasion, I went to the sawmill with Uncle—I liked to climb the stacks of lumber—I always took King with me. Queenie recognized me, but she and King were strangers. I was horrified once when I saw him try to mount her, but she, not being in heat, simply evaded him.

King went everywhere with me—into town, into the woods, on the creek. He learned quickly to sit quietly in a boat. I don't think he had to learn; King was born knowing a lot of things other dogs have to learn. Uncle hadn't bought me a boat yet, but I was always free to use Lamar's, with or without Lamar. I've never known anyone freer with the few possessions he had.

Often the three of us glided along the creek, coming in to a sand bar or a mudbank here and there to explore. More often it was King in the front of the boat, leaning forward like a figurehead on a clipper ship, so eager was he to see what came next—me in the back using the paddle quietly.

With me at first, later by himself, King went everywhere and all over town. Everyone knew him. He was an independent dog, but friendly, too. He liked the company of people as much as he liked his own company, or the company of woods and creek. I have found him sitting perfectly contented with a group of men at the barbershop or in front of the bank or on the wooden platform of the depot, seeming to enjoy their talk. He never, of course, knew the feel of leash or halter. All his life he was free.

He made acceptance of me in the town easier than it might have been. He was my dog and they all knew it. The women of the town wanted at first to cluck over me with pity because I had been orphaned, and this naturally put up the backs of their menfolk. The children, in spite of the fact that I was sponsored by the impeccably trustworthy Lamar and Johnny-May, distrusted me as a city boy who might try to put on airs. Even the facts that Uncle and Aunt had no children of their own and that Uncle was one of the big men in that town worked against me. But the other fact, that King was my dog, made a place for me. If I were shy, if my accent sounded funny and different to them—well, it was easy to pat my dog and go from that to little jokes with me. We got to be known together. If they saw mc without King they'd say, "Where's King?" I found out that if they saw King without me, they'd say, "Where's the boy?"

I knew instinctively that I needed the town, not just Uncle and Aunt. But it was because of King that I found it easy to exchange greetings and teasing with the men, the loungers who make town gossip and often town opinion, as much as the women who rock and sew together and talk. We lived out of the common way, so few children came to see me, and when they did, well—"He can't play, he has to practice!" Behind my back at school I heard them mimic Aunt more than once. The truth is that outside of school, where I enjoyed them, I seldom sought the companionship of other children. I lived a busy life what with school, Lamar across the road—mostly King and the woods and the fields. There was never as much time to be out there as I wanted.

(I suddenly remember, for no reason I know, a particular late afternoon in autumn. King walking beside me as we climb a hilly field toward a farmhouse. King with sudden high spirits racing ahead to greet somebody in the yard. Our standing a few minutes later by a persimmon tree, talking to somebody and sampling a ripe persimmon.)

It was the piano practice and having been a city boy that kept me from acceptance. If Aunt had known, I'm sure she would not have insisted on the piano. But she did not know, and I could not tell her that some of the boys thought me sissy.

It was because of King that they changed their minds. The Caldwells were butchering a cow and a heifer one day, and such an event was sure to draw all the boys and unoccupied men of the town. King had taken to waiting for me after school under a chinaberry tree overlooking the school grounds. That afternoon I decided to brave Aunt's disapproval and cut piano practice, so King and I went along with the other boys to the Caldwells'. The cow and heifer had been killed and skinned and hung up to drain on great hooks projecting from the door of the barn. But the center of interest had passed from them to a bull in a large pen.

Men sat high on the fence surrounding the pen, taunting the understandably enraged bull inside. He had seen, he had heard, he had smelled. He knew that his kind, indeed his *own*, had been killed. Along with other boys I climbed up beside the men to watch, not really wanting to, feeling pity for the bull, but having to because that's what the men were doing.

So I laughed with them when I didn't feel like laughing,

and I forgot King. He was almost, not quite, grown then. He had all of his size but not yet all of his muscle, nor quite all of his learning.

With the others I watched the bull charge the fence where we sat. With them I braced myself, held my legs out of danger, and laughed. Then I saw King in the pen with the bull. He had taken his excitement from the people he trusted. He barked, challenging the bull. The ringleader of the loungers, a man named Toll Weaver, stupid and laughing at the sight of the little dog and the big bull, yelled, "Sic him!"

King barked again and charged the bull. The bull, surprised, drew back. Encouraged, King charged again with ferocious barking, bravely, foolishly showing off. The bull lowered his head. King stood his ground, growling low and threateningly. The men whooped with laughter.

As the bull drew himself back to charge, I dropped from the fence to the ground. The drop stunned me for an instant but I was able to grab my dog and throw him up toward the fence. One of the men, surprised, caught him, as men will try to catch anything thrown at them. I turned, I don't know why, to face the bull. But before I had turned fully, one of the bull's horns, aimed low to rip the dog, caught me in the calf of a leg.

Men who a moment before had been laughing promptly jumped from the fence into the pen. With shouts and waving arms they drove the bull away. I was lifted up to other hands on the fence, my leg streaming blood. Other hands caught me and lifted me down on the other side. I was laid on the ground almost fainting. King twisted anxiously, licking my face and whining.

A couple of men set off running to bring a doctor. Another picked me up and carried me and King home in his car.

The doctor had to take fourteen stitches in my leg, and I was excused from school and piano practice for two weeks. I was very happy. People said such pleasant things. I was a brave boy, I was a hero. I enjoyed the praise quite immodestly, although I was careful to keep a modest face. When, eventually, I made it into town, I cultivated a slight limp which drew sympathetic attention to me until that fool fifteen-year-old girl got hysterics in the drugstore one day. She screamed out that she was hopelessly in love with the science teacher in high school and tried to drink a bottle of iodine. The science teacher's wife was in the drugstore at the time and slapped the girl good and hard, upsetting the bottle of iodine which spilled down the fool girl's dress. Then both of them had hysterics and had to be given spirits of ammonia and led off to their homes by separate delighted and scandalized factions. *That* gave the town something new to talk about, and I knew after that I might as well walk like anybody else.

Before I was on my feet King gave up most of his private excursions and stayed by me wherever I lay or sat. One rule of Aunt's was relaxed at this time and never again enforced. That was that King was not to sleep with me. Spoiled as I was at this time, I was allowed to have my way. Aunt did not give me permission, but she ignored the unmistakable signs left by King's dirty feet on the sheets. He often went off on night prowls by himself as I lay in bed reading. When he returned, his growl at the door was low and discreet. I was out of bed and letting him in fast to keep him from making another sound.

He made for the bed and settled himself under the

covers, if it was cold. I joined him, clasping him lightly about the chest. His coat was cool and smelled of the outside. When it got too warm for him, he'd get out from under the covers, make two or three turns, and settle down on the top quilt, always close to me. Sometimes he dreamed. His feet would twitch and kick as if he were chasing something. I could feel his muzzle move and hear him snuffle a dream-bark as he ran after who knows what friend or foe in the woods.

Early as I rose, he was always awake before me. He never tried to paw me awake. But I often opened my eyes to see King on the floor beside the bed, looking at me with interest and expectation. In a minute we were out in the air together, across the field, down to the woods and the creek.

Chapter 4

Aunt and King did not quite love each other, but they did have mutual respect. Uncle didn't have much to do with him yet, just let him grow. Aunt fed him and taught him he was one of many animals on the place. Of course he was not just that and he knew it, but he had to learn to let live. When he chased the chickens, she caught him and gave him a few quick smacks. When he barked at the hogs or the cows, she gave him a sound kick and a finger-shaking scolding. When he tried to engage the dainty appalled Mildred in a game of rough and tumble, it was explained to him by Aunt with fists on hips and eyes on fire that Mildred was neither a rubber ball nor a stone.

Very soon, for he learned quickly, he walked peaceably among the yard fowls without causing a flutter; he kept a respectful distance from the cows; he ceased barking at the hogs, contenting himself with sitting outside their pen and hassling at them broodingly.

King and Tom had some good chases together. Tom had come to inspect the pups the morning after they were born, and having satisfied himself that they were not rats, thereafter treated them as playfellows. Even Mildred, after her early displeasure at his bad puppy manners, accepted him. I have seen him lying on his side in the sun, exhausted after an active adventure, and seen Mildred pick her way down the back steps and into the yard where he lay, stare at him with frowning disapproval, and then curl up and sleep beside him as if he were another cat.

This was especially remarkable, because as King matured he seemed to have an inborn hatred of cats and killed them when they crossed him, thereby causing us all a lot of worry and trouble. But Tom and Mildred—after Aunt taught him—were different. They were *our* cats. He accepted them, even loved them, I think. At least once he went to Mildred's defense.

She had in her indifferent, privileged way allowed herself on one of her walks of inspection to be trapped in a corner of the yard by a fierce, mean-tempered turkey gobbler Aunt was fattening for the table. Mildred had the look on her face of a lady who discovers there is a mouse loose in the room and looks for but finds no chair to stand on. She was shocked, offended, and terribly frightened, enough to make her let go an unaccustomed wail for help.

King and I, who had been playing a game of throw and fetch with a piece of firewood, ran toward the sound and got there as the turkey made a full-sail pass at Mildred's eyes. King was on the turkey and broke his neck with one furious shake. Mildred streaked for the kitchen. In a minute Aunt streaked from it, in time to see the bested gobbler sink to his knees and expire. She gave King an automatic cuff before I could explain what had happened. Then Aunt philosophically boiled a pot of water and plucked the turkey, which we ate the next couple of days. To repay his favor Mildred agreeably shared a plate of giblets with King, and Aunt, not much one to pet animals, reached down in the midst of her cooking to give each of them an approving stroke.

The thing Aunt and King could not see eye to eye on was baths. Being white, he showed dirt easily, and there was no telling when Aunt would decide the time had come to bathe him. The kettle of water would go on the stove with a clang at an odd hour of the afternoon, after which Aunt would set a washtub squarely in the middle of the yard. King would by now have seen the mene, mene, tekel on the wall and skulked under the house. Aunt would say to me, "Get him."

And I would have to crawl under the house (Southern houses seldom had cellars then; they were set on short piles of brick or stone) to find King. I would call to him in my most cajoling Judas tone, but he knew when I was not master of my own fate, let alone his; and he crawled on his belly and hid in any dark place he could find. Curiously, he never ran for the woods, he always went under the house. It was as if really running away would have violated a certain rule of the game. On the other hand, he wasn't going to encourage Aunt by making it easy for her.

When I found him and dragged him out by a hind leg, he groaned and muttered at me, but never offered to snap. It was dead weight I dragged, inch by inch, getting myself dirtier than King was. I would have to follow his bath with one of my own.

In the end he was docile. He allowed himself to be

lifted—Aunt and I each with a hand clutching a leg—into the tub of hot water. At this point Aunt grew aggressively cheerful. As she soaped his body and head with coarse brown laundry soap, which she herself made in a three-legged black pot in the yard, she would say, "Nice dog, good dog, *clean* dog!" King stared ahead with tortured impassivity, the way I have imagined Joan at the stake.

When Aunt had rinsed him in a soapy rinse from the same tub, she gave him the signal, "*All* right!" and he jumped out. First he shook himself as dry as he could, and then he rolled himself in the nearest loose dirt he could find, before loping off with as much dignity as he could muster to the woods. He would forgive me for my complicity in the event, but it would take a few hours.

The bath done, Aunt was as jolly as a Christian who has just saved a heathen from hell's fire. She would empty and rinse the tub and put it away. And she would say to me, "I think *you'd* better give yourself a bath before supper." That night King and I would go to bed more or less clean, although he generally smelled of the creek he'd swum in after his bath to try to get rid of the smell of soap.

During this time, the time of my mending leg, two things of importance happened. I acquired a new pet, and King acquired, not a new master, but a new pursuit. The new pet was a pig I called Noochy—every animal I knew had to have a name. King's new pursuit was hunting. Uncle took him out to try him, found that he had natural aptitude, and set about teaching him the finer points of stalking, flushing, and retrieving. Pretty soon Uncle or Lamar was taking him out with the gun almost every day for an hour or two.

Hunting was one of the few activities that King and I did not share. When I got older, I learned to shoot, and I liked practicing with a target or a tin can set on a fence post, but I could not aim a gun at a bird or a rabbit and squeeze the trigger. Uncle saw something illogical in this, since I was as quick as anyone to enjoy game when it was served up at mealtime. But kill it I could not.

One other way I never became a real country boy was fishing. I tried it. Lamar showed me how to make a bait bed, gave me a start of worms from his own bait bed, and for a while I kept it properly damped down. But fishing just plain bored me, and I never developed any skill at it. I suppose if I'd pulled up a fish every time I dropped a line in the water I'd have thought it tolerable fun. But a real fisherman can spend a day relaxed on the bank of a stream, losing his bait to wily old fish, fouling his hooks on submerged roots, getting rained on, never catching a thing—and at the end of such a day still feel that he's had a good time. When different pleasures took us different ways, there was no jealousy or grudging on King's part or mine; we were completely sure of each other.

One of the times King was off hunting I, idle and wanting amusement, hobbled into the yard and down to the hogpen. When they saw me coming, they came running, for if pigs mean food to people, people also mean food to pigs, although certainly in a different way. When they saw I had no slops or corn, they wandered off, all except one little pig. I climbed up and sat on the top of the fence, hooking my heels on a lower plank for steadiness. The pig looked up at me grunting. His ears crooked attentively, and his soft, gray-pink snout twitched. "Hello, Noochy," I said.

Noochy was the closest I could come to the sound he was making.

When I spoke, his grunts became more rapid, as if he were answering me. We contemplated each other quietly then for a while, until I clambered down inside the pen. He did not run away. I squatted on my heels, and he came right up to me. I put out a hand. He sniffed it with his damp snout. I scratched him gently and rhythmically behind the ears, and he recommenced his pleased grunting.

What is it that makes an occasional domestic animal, one in a thousand maybe, want to be friends with a human being? I don't know, but I've known it to happen with cows and mules and even once with a flighty guinea cock.

I scratched his back, and he gave his tail a twirl, and I laughed. He looked at me with his small jaws open, almost as if he were smiling, pleased to have pleased me. I don't remember whether it was later that day or the next that I visited Noochy again, but soon we were old friends. I took to opening the gate a crack and letting him out with me. He didn't run away. I knew he wouldn't. He just wanted to be with me.

Together we walked slowly through the yard—or I walked slowly, and he bucked along in short bursts, then stood waiting for me to catch up. This was more than the nerves of the silly chickens could bear. They scattered before us and set up a clamor that brought Aunt to the back door to investigate. She stared at us for a moment and then threw her apron over her face, laughing and bending forward. "If you don't look a sight!" she cried. "You and that pig walking like he was a dog or a cat!" Then the impropriety struck her. "Did you let him out?"

"Yes'm."

"He'll run away!"

"No, he won't.'

"You'll have to catch him if he does, with your poor leg, too—"

"He won't run away."

Noochy looked from her to me, concentrating finally on me as the giver and arbiter of his freedom.

"Better put him back, boy."

"He won't run away. I promise, Aunt."

She paused. "Well, put him back when you get tired of him. I've got a pie in the oven." She turned briskly and went back into the kitchen, letting the door slam behind her.

In a few seconds she was back. "You be good now and I won't tell your uncle." She went to the kitchen again.

Why had she said that? I wondered. Why would Uncle care?

But he did care when he found out a day or two later. My strolls with Noochy had become so common that he was spending about as much of his daytime life out of the pen as he did in it. After initial surprise Tom and King accepted him as one of us. Tom lifted a paw tentatively and touched Noochy's jaw, and Noochy simply grunted in a friendly way. I actually saw King, more times than one, scratching Noochy's stomach as Noochy lay on his side snuffling with pleasure. Of the pets only Mildred would not accept him. On her lady-of-the-manor tours of the grounds, when she saw Tom, King, Noochy, and me just being amiable together, she cut us as dead as a good woman cutting a known whore on the street.

When Uncle knew, he was disturbed. "It's a bad idea," he told Aunt.

By then Aunt was a pleader for my cause. "He gets lonesome. He needs something new to do—when you take King off hunting. It'll be all right when his leg heals and he goes back to school. He'll forget and be doing other things. But let him, now!"

Unwillingly, fighting his own natural kindness, Uncle acquiesced. But he was right, as things turned out, as they had to. When I went back to school and the hated piano, I did not forget Noochy. He had become one of mine, and every day I found a time for him. More, when spring turned into summer, and I was free of school and the piano. He had a special greedy love for pears, and when the pear tree bore fruit, before the fruit was ripe, I gathered pears and took them to Noochy, who ate the green things as if they were ambrosia.

I don't like to tell it, but I guess I have to. It became a story that was told more often on me than by me—that recital near the end of the school year! As the black day, or evening, came nearer, I was even more firmly held to my practice than I had been before. Aunt had bragged to the ladies of the town that I was to play a piece. I tried, oh, I did try, but I could never get it right, that aggravating "Over the Candy Counter." Scales were abandoned. I concentrated on the piece. But I could never make it sound better than a punishment for sinners.

However, Aunt and Miss Spiers were bound and determined. Aunt had to believe in miracles if she thought it would go off well, or even adequately. As for Miss Spiers, her professional reputation was at stake. She had promised to have me playing that piece by the end of the term, and I *would!* What neither she nor Aunt took into account was me.

On the night we had our supper even earlier than usual, and it was generally about six. I took a bath and put on my blue suit. King sat in my room, following every movement, listening to my complaints and threats with such unconcerned amusement that I finally turned on him and declared, "Well, *you* don't have to do it!"

Uncle wore a suit, too, although the weather was already hot. Aunt was corseted, fluffed, and powdered within an inch of her life. We drove off in the Ford, Uncle and I grim, Aunt all abubble with false assurance and gaiety.

When we got to the schoolhouse, I was taken backstage of the auditorium by Aunt and given into the charge of Miss Spiers. The sight of the other children made me feel weak. They were all dressed up in a way I'd never seen them before, even at church or birthday parties. Some of them looked glumly determined. Some of them looked even as if they *enjoyed* the chance to show off. One awful little girl I used to thwack on the head with a pencil when I passed her in the halls sat with her pink taffeta dress and her little black curls all in place, white shoes spotless, hands quietly folded in her lap, looking as if it were the happiest moment of her life. I wanted to put an arrow through her.

I sidled over and peeked around the curtain, something we'd all been warned not to do. Oh, God! There they all were, all the people I knew—Uncle looking like a murderer trying to be brave at his execution, Aunt flushed and chattering with friends around her—even Aunt May and Lamar and Johnny-May. They were sitting in the front row, having arrived early; Johnny-May had her bloomers on and looked as clean and as dead as a china doll.

The recital began. When my turn came and Miss Spiers pinched my arm and pushed me forward to go onto the stage, I balked. I said no, and finding I could say no I said it again and again until she, aware of and flustered by the restlessness of the audience, passed over me and went on to the next one.

But Aunt, knowing the order of the program, was soon backstage. When Miss Spiers explained the situation to her, her first reaction was to take me by the shoulders and shake me. She had never before touched me with anger, or even annoyance. The more she threatened and begged and shook me, the firmer became my resolve. She said I was a disappointment to her and Miss Spiers and to Uncle. She tried to bribe me with favors.

"No! I can't and I won't!"

"You're just nervous. Miss Spiers says she'll put you at the end. Won't that be all right?"

"I'm not nervous or scared. I just won't because I'm not good enough."

It was a great discovery, that I did not have to say yes, that I could say no to anything I was that unwilling to do. Finally she gave up. The recital ended, and I was taken home in disgrace. Only Uncle seemed cheerful, and he was pretty cautious about it.

Poor Aunt. It must have been a dreadful night for her. Before we left the schoolhouse I heard her telling people that I was just not feeling well and she thought I had a fever and might be coming down with one of those bad summer colds. She fervently promised, as if they cared, that

I would play in the recital next year. I knew I would not. Even Aunt, I think, realized that I was not to have the career in music she had once dreamed of for her little girl. The piano stood closed until I was adolescent and young people came to parties. There were always one or two willing to play for the rest of us to dance.

Miss Spiers, when we passed each other in the halls at school after that, would neither look at me nor speak to me, just sail on by with her lips pinched tight and her chin up in the air. I had failed her; I was a blot on her record.

Chapter 5

GOOD THOUGH life was in that town, it would be a lie to pretend there were no warts or sores. There were ignorance and prejudice and jealousy and in some measure probably all the vices and evils to be found in a larger place. There was very little privacy, there were very few secrets. Everybody knew one of our doctors took dope, but when he was steady people swore by him. It ended by his going crazy one day and killing his wife for no reason anybody knew. She was hanging out her washing on the clothesline. He shot her through the heart and then went into the kitchen and shot himself through the head.

There were a few flirty married women in town who caused trouble from time to time, and everybody knew which girls did and which didn't, just as everybody knew which men "ran around." The distinction was carefully drawn between a man who drank and a man who would take a drink.

A minor example of town prejudice was that against me when I first came there to live because I was a city boy. A major example was the prejudice much of the town felt against a Yankee family who had settled there. I didn't know about it until many years later after I'd gone away and then come back. Mrs. Belser told me then and seemed surprised I hadn't known. I'd always thought the Belsers were like everybody else, except that they talked different, which I liked because it gave us variety and a hint of other places. But Mrs. Belser said that when she and her husband had wanted to settle there and open an icehouse and little novelty shop, nobody would sell them a store or any land to build on.

They'd been traveling with a carnival looking for just such a town as ours to live in. They were not performers; that wasn't what counted against them. They had merely held the cotton-candy and candied-apple concession. What counted against them was that they were Yankees. It was Uncle who helped them. He heard of their problem, talked it over with them. He owned no town property he could sell them, so he bought a place and resold it to them.

A lot of people in town felt betrayed, and some of them hated Uncle for what he had done. For a time they wouldn't trade with the Belsers, but when the first summer came, their desire for ice overcame their resentment of the Yankees. Before, they'd had to fetch their ice from a town five miles away; they'd drive over in groups and bring it back standing on the wide running board cars had then. Half the ice would be melted before they got it home. After they bought ice from the Belsers, they bought other things. It was a wonderful little store Mrs. Belser ran.

Everybody went there to buy presents for birthday parties and bridal showers and any impractical knickknack the bigger stores thought it foolish or uneconomical to stock. Two or three times a year Mrs. Belser got on the train by herself and went off to Savannah or Atlanta to buy her variety.

I think one of the ties of sympathy between my people and the Belsers was that the Belsers had no children of their own, and Uncle and Aunt knew something about that. In any event, Aunt never went to town without stopping a few minutes to chat with Mrs. Belser, whether she had anything to buy or not, and she told me to do the same. I needed no encouragement to be friendly with the Belsers. They had so many funny and interesting stories to tell about carnival life and carnival people. I could have spent all day just looking at all the pretty things they had in the shop. And Mr. Belser never let me leave without giving me a piece of candy.

The town five miles away from us looked down on us because it was twice as big, and we looked down on the next town in the other direction because it was only half our size. Picayune, silly. But I don't notice New York and London and Tokyo ignoring the question of which is largest. It would seem logical to think that big is big and little is little, and let it go, but it doesn't work out that way.

When I speak of prejudice, I don't intend to hit on color prejudice, at least not very much. What would be called color prejudice today was then an accepted social order. It may hurt to admit it, but nothing is gained by pretending that the Emperor is fully dressed when he's standing there naked as a light bulb. I played with Negro children, but I didn't go to school with them, and they were not invited to the parties I went to and gave. Aunt and Uncle did not create the social order they lived in. Neither did they try to change it. Not everybody is a revolutionary, especially if he holds some of the good cards in the deck. Revolution has a more natural appeal to the underdog than it has to the overdog. If you expect the privileged to show much enthusiasm for giving up their privileges, you're in for disappointment. But if anybody said to me Aunt and Uncle were a jot less than good people ought to be, they'd have me to fight.

The warts and sores were there, sometimes plain for all to see, sometimes hidden. But there was a goodness of sharing and a neighborliness in the town that are rare in larger places. If somebody's house burned down, the next day he'd find everybody else in town giving or lending him a bed, a chair, a stove, a sheet, a quilt, a pan, a place. If there was sickness or death, all the women helped, or offered to. When there was a wedding, everybody went. Also, looking back now, it seems to me there was a remarkable tolerance of eccentricity, so long as that eccentricity had been born to the town.

Summer had come. School was out, and the lovely fiery days seemed to stretch endlessly ahead. The boys of the town went everywhere and did everything. Because there were fewer of us than in a city, any group of us was likely to contain boys of different ages. Sometimes the boy groups and the girl groups mingled for a particular activity, but mostly they went about separate business until dating age.

There were the two trains to be met every day, and sometimes the thrill of exchanging words with those great men, the engineers. Or we might stand in a field and wave at the hoboes on a passing freight. They always waved back. We thought them romantic beings, envied them their freedom of movement. They put us in mind of joining a circus or running away to join the Navy and lead a sailor's life. For the land-bound, country-town boy, the sea always sounds a special call, and more than one of us answered it.

A mile up the railroad tracks were the remains of an Indian settlement with its burying ground, and we often tramped up there to look for arrowheads and bits of pottery. I still have some of these. I take them out and look at them occasionally to this day. There was an especially rich growth of scuppernong vines in the tall trees up near the Indian place, and late summer often found us high in the branches of the trees, gorging ourselves on the tough-skinned, grape-like scuppernongs. Aunt used them to make jelly, just as she did the plums and blackberries we found in the woods and beside the roads. On many of our tramps we carried clean syrup buckets to gather berries and plums that grew in such abundance.

There was the trash dump to be visited and sifted for treasure. Other people's throwaways are always more interesting than our own. I remember one day Lamar had all of us boys laughing when he found a busted corset and held it around him, aping a fine lady's walk. Even if we found only tin cans, we could put them to use. Lamar taught me to punch holes in the sides, string them with long wire, the ends of which we held in our hands when we walked on the cans. We fancied that we looked like Japanese in their stilt shoes.

Or there were the light chores. No boy likes them. He is always too busy to do them. But I did my share of picking peas, of bringing drinking water from the artesian well, of cutting grass and feeding hogs. Going to get the ice was the chore I minded least, because it afforded me a visit with the Belsers. I admired Mr. Belser's skill at chipping off just the right-sized piece with his sharp pick and deftly tying a cord around it so that I could carry it. I always bought a dime's worth, which was enough to ice our tea for dinner and supper and have enough left over to cool the milk and butter. I recall the delightful coolness of the ice against my thigh as I lugged it home. It left a wet patch on the side of my shorts or overalls.

There were few electric refrigerators in town then, and those were all in the stores. The town's source of electricity was unreliable. The mildest thunderstorm could put the lights out. That's why Aunt always kept kerosene lamps at the ready. One of my chores was to clean the glass flues with wadded newspaper while Aunt trimmed the wicks.

Sometimes King and I went out to the farms or to the sawmill with Uncle. At the mill there were the stacks of fresh lumber to climb. I frequently came away with resin and small splinters in my hands and feet. And there were the men to watch as they sawed away, to beg to let me try their chewing tobacco, which always smelled so good in the open air. And there was the sinister, evil-looking equipment that cut the logs into planks.

On the farms there were the children, black and white, to make friends with. We often found them working in the fields with their fathers and mothers. I learned to chop cotton by taking over a hoe now and then as we talked. One little girl I fell in love with. She was my first love, and she was black as midnight. She was shy, and her dimples showed when she smiled, and I thought her the most beautiful thing I had ever seen. Her name was Tussy.

On my second trip to Tussy's farm I bravely, blushingly carried a note, which I pressed into her hand only when we were about to leave. It read "I love you do you love me." The next time we visited the farm Tussy pressed into *my* hand a note just before we left—pressed it into my hand and ran away from the car, around to the back of the house. The note read "I love you do you love me." All summer we gazed at each other on those visits, wordlessly, hopelessly in love, and always we exchanged those notes that read just the same. Uncle was aware of our innocent child passion, but he never let me know. I guessed only when—but that can wait its time.

The center of our lives during the summer was the Milly Hole, the place where the creek was wider and deeper than anywhere else near the town. The only explanation of its name I ever heard was dirty, but the truth was nobody knew why it was called that, and quite proper ladies used the name in conversation.

The longer way was across the bridge, along the hot dirt road until it forked, along the right fork until it hit a path between the cotton gin and the colored church. (Across the road from the gin was a pine-wooded slope which Uncle owned; gypsies camped there one whole winter.) The short way was to cross the bridge and at a certain spot everyone knew to plunge from the road down its steep bank and follow a path through high weeds, a path that could be felt with the feet better than seen, even when you were on it. Women and girls (except Johnny-May) took the longer way generally. Men and boys went the shorter, sometimes running and whooping because snakes were said to frequent the path.

When it was only men and boys at the Milly Hole we went in bare. But we usually carried along our bathing suits to slip on in case a group of girls and women came along. They knew to stop at the last bend before the creek and call out. If there was no answer, they went ahead. If we were there, we'd shout back for them to wait a minute till we got decent. Sometimes we kept them waiting for the fun of it. If they suspected this, one of them would shout that they were coming ready or not. And giggling they would approach. Any butt that was still bare would streak for its clothes or swimming suit. We changed our clothes in the woods on the bank, and often when we dressed again we carried red bugs with us that would itch like the devil for a few hours.

There was a cable stretched across the creek, and on it a short length of pipe. It was great fun to clasp the pipe and ride it down into the creek. It took a strong arm to shoot it back for the next rider. There was a big log across the narrowest end of the Milly Hole, submerged a few inches under water. We used to swim to it and sit on it, the water lapping just over our thighs and privates. It was at the Milly Hole, of course, that boys saw each other nude and had occasion to compare shape and size, to count the hairs on their chests, and to brag about that, if any, around the genitals. I was the only boy in town who had been circumcized, but this embarrassment of mine was passed over sympathetically by the other boys, to whom it was a particular horror that any part of them should be lost.

At the beginning of the summer I could not swim. I paddled tirelessly in the shallows with my feet touching bottom, but all Lamar's advice and instruction availed naught. He was at a loss to teach me, because he couldn't remember a time when he couldn't swim. It was Uncle who settled the matter.

We were all there one Saturday afternoon early in summer, Uncle, Aunt, and I wearing almost identically designed one-piece bathing suits with short skirts. When he'd had his first swim and come back to the sand bar to rest, Uncle found me paddling in the shallows. There must have been fifty people in swimming that day, laughing and splashing, doing "watch the moon rise" and playing water tag, ducking one another. King and a couple of bird dogs were there, too, swimming with the people and enjoying themselves.

Uncle asked me why I wasn't out sitting on the log with the other boys, and I admitted to him that I couldn't swim. He frowned, waded out, and scooped me up. Turning with me in the water, as if to wind himself up, he presently let me go. I found myself flying out across the water—Uncle was lean, but he was strong—and when I hit the water I sank. But I rose, and I found myself swimming.

Aunt, who had observed only the last moment of the event, flew at Uncle, weeping, and beat him on the chest with her fists. He held her off laughing. Swallowing and spitting water as I was, I managed to cry, "I can swim! I can swim!"

After that there was no holding me. Lamar quickly taught me the overhand stroke, and I jeered at King for his dog paddling that I had so recently used.

Early in the morning, soon after breakfast, I'd go to the Milly Hole to practice, with only King, in spite of Aunt's warning never to go into the water for two hours after eating. The Milly Hole was deserted and quiet then; I had it all to myself. It was a little scary. The sounds of hidden birds, the croak of a frog, the plop of a turtle into water could make me jump and look over my shoulder. It was those times that made me understand that although we could use the creek and think it belonged to us, it belonged to nobody. It would be there when we were dust and the Milly Hole a forgotten place where nobody came but the birds and the snakes and the small woodland animals.

The only thing lacking those mornings was that I could not use the pipe on the cable. If it happened to be up when I got there, I could fly down once, but I hadn't the strength to send the pipe back hard enough so that it would stick fast on the short level of cable that had been made for it. The log confused King. I could sit on it comfortably, the cool brown water trickling under and over my legs when I raised or lowered them. But the log was too slippery and rounded for King to sit on, however much both of us tried to settle him. Eventually he gave it up and swam back to the bank to wait for me. I had some of my deepest and happiest thoughts sitting alone on the log at the Milly Hole early in the morning. King never hurried me, never grew impatient. He made side excursions into the woods, returning now and then to see if I was ready to go.

Sometimes an early swimming party would arrive before I left, and I would stay with them awhile. Mostly I swam alone, or with King, and I became a good swimmer. When I came out I would, still wet, slip into my shorts or overalls and steal away, not reluctantly, feeling that I had been something of an intruder, giving silent thanks to the creek for allowing me to come and go with no harm.

As summer progressed, the point of interest for the boys became not the Milly Hole but the wooden bridge that led to it. The creek was low, the bridge stood high. There had not been much rain, except in Tussy's part of the county, and there it seemed to rain almost every day. Good for the corn to begin with. Bad for the corn later, and for the cotton, and for the people.

The bridge drew us like a magnet. We'd stand and stare from it down at the creek, the color of unpolished brass because of the lack of rain, the dirt and clay it traveled over turning it darker, almost black in the shade of trees.

Sometimes I stood by myself and looked down at the creek from the bridge. More often I did it in company.

"I dare you."

"I dare *you!*"

"I double-dog dare you!"

No boy had ever jumped from the bridge to the creek, and none did now.

But one day when I was there with Lamar and Johnny-May and a few of the town boys and we were going through our pattern of daring each other, I said, "I will!" I don't know why I said it, and as soon as I'd said it, I wished I hadn't. But I had said it. They waited, soundless jeers on their lips, disbelief changing to belief in their eyes. Then I had to do it.

I jumped. A second later King jumped after me. I landed with a smack, my body sideways, and my head hitting the water. I sank numbed, forever and ever and ever; I rose slowly. When my head broke the surface, the first thing I saw was King's head, looking anxiously about. He swam toward me, and together we made our way to the bank, ignoring the shouts of the boys and Johnny-May on the bridge. I was still a little stunned as they scrambled down the steep bank and escorted me home. I gave no answer to their questions and exclamations, and I made them leave me, even Lamar and Johnny-May, at the gate to the back yard, my commonest entry. Aunt asked me how I'd got my clothes wet; I told her I'd fallen into the creek.

But the boys went home and told their mothers, in order, I suspected, to get their mothers to forbid them to do it ever, under any circumstances. Of course word got to Aunt by nightfall. I'd kept out of her way pretty much after getting into dry clothes, but I always loved standing at the kitchen door, watching her fly around getting supper. I thought it wouldn't do to break habit, so there I was. Uncle had brought home a mess of fish that day and scaled and gutted them for our supper. Aunt stood dipping a small perch into corn meal on both sides. Then she held it by the tail and shook loose meal off it before dropping it into the frying pan. Presently she turned and looked me directly in the eye.

"Did you jump off the bridge like they say?"

"Yes'm."

"Well." She took a deep breath, decided not to panic. "Don't ever do it again, you hear?"

"Yes'm."

"You promise now?"

"Yes'm," I said. Gratefully.

Chapter 6

THERE WAS, as Aunt said to Uncle, "a lot more to Lamar than he lets on." Not only was he good at his schoolbooks, but he was smart in a lot of practical ways and clever with anything mechanical. Show him how something worked one time and the next time he knew. He could take anything apart and put it back together and not have pieces left over, as I generally did.

Lamar brooded on life. He was friendly, but he had a lot of reserve in him, too. One of the reasons he liked me and King, aside from the fact that we lived across the road (which is no guarantee), was that we liked being with him but we knew when to leave him alone. Uncle was his hero; anybody could see that. But there were times he acted as if he couldn't stand the sight of any of us.

I studied about it a long time before I came up with an answer. He was jealous of us, and he was ashamed of his own family. Not Johnny-May—he knew she had character. But Aunt May was about as near nothing as a person could be, one of those weak, whiny women who can't do a thing right. She wasn't even a good cook. Looking at those two smart children of hers made you wonder about heredity. Knowing Aunt May, you didn't wonder why her husband had left her; you marveled that she'd been able to get one in the first place and keep him long enough to hatch two chicks. If it hadn't been that woman at the ball game at Wrens, it would have been somebody else. I never knew him, of course, but how could he be bad if he was father to Lamar and Johnny-May Salter?

And there was the added thing that, although he'd run away with another woman, he still sent money to his first family. He wasn't the first man nor the last to make the mistake of his life because a pretty face smiled at him. The thing that gnawed at Lamar was that he felt his daddy had run away from him and Johnny-May as well as his mama. I don't think he gave much of a damn about the money. Young as he was, he could have gone to work and supported that family if he'd had to.

No, it wasn't that. It was that he wanted and needed a daddy, one like Uncle. I think part of the reason he forgave me Uncle was that Uncle wasn't *my* father either, although he acted like a father to both of us boys, even as Aunt was about to take over with Johnny-May and teach her things she should have learned from her mother.

One Saturday Uncle took Lamar and me in the car all the way to Swainsboro to see a new picture called *Wings*. Lamar just fell in love with airplanes then and there. There was another reason than seeing *Wings*, although that would have been enough. On the way back, after he'd filled us up with ice cream, Uncle stopped at a place over near Wadley where a fellow actually *had* a plane, his own plane, which he kept in his own field, and would take people up in for fifteen minutes for seven dollars and a half each.

"You boys like to go up?" Uncle asked offhandedly after we had inspected the plane.

"Yes, sir!" I said without hesitation, and the only reason Lamar hesitated was that he knew what it cost. But you could tell by the way his eyes flared up that Lamar would give up his chance to go to heaven for a ride in that plane.

"All right," Uncle said, and paid the man.

King had been with us all day; Uncle made him stay in the car only when we were inside the picture show. He watched us scramble up to the back seat, squeezing in together, and he watched the aviator climb into his seat in front. The aviator had showed Uncle how to twirl the propeller. He twirled it, and away we went.

Later, Uncle told us King had just watched at first with mild surprise. He was, after all, used to seeing people crank up a car and roll off in it. But when we left the ground and sailed up into the air, Uncle said King sat back on his haunches and howled, thinking, I suppose, that we had gone up to heaven in both ways.

There's no describing that ride, and no need to. People are so used to planes these days there's little thrill in it. But then, for the first time, to be—up! The wind whipped our faces white, and I'm only surprised we didn't die then and there from sheer excitement. I was too busy with my own feelings to think about Lamar, but I know that what I felt he must have felt a hundredfold. It was like being God, up there in the Infinite, looking down at the matchbox houses and buglike cattle and people. Lamar had loved Uncle before, but now there was nothing he wouldn't have done for him.

Aunt kicked up a fuss when she heard about it, but by then there was nothing she could do. King was just dumbfounded that I returned at all, and for days wouldn't let me out of his sight.

It's hard to calculate time so long after, but it was probably no more than a week or two later, that the Salters got word that Mr. Salter was dead. He'd died of a heart attack watching a ball game in the hot sun. As one of the loungers at the barbershop was heard to say, "Watching ball games was just pure-and-T bad luck for that fellow."

Lamar came over and told us. It wasn't bad enough that he had died, but *she,* the woman he'd run off with, said she was his wife and that she was bringing him back to his home town to bury him, because that had always been his expressed wish. Aunt went right off to Aunt May's to look after her and Johnny-May and make sure they had decent clothes for the funeral.

Uncle studied about the whole thing for a long time, frowning, while Lamar just stood there looking at him. Finally he made up his mind. Slapping his thigh to signal this, he said, "All right. I have to do something you're not going to like, Lamar. I have to meet her—and your daddy—and I have to look after her while she's here. Maybe she's his wife like she says and maybe she isn't, but somebody has to. You see that. It's for your daddy."

Lamar's face was awful with betrayal. "No, sir! I don't see! You mean you're going to treat her like his *wife* with Mama and us *there?*"

"Lamar—"

"You and me ain't friends no more!" Lamar declared, choking, and ran out of the house.

Uncle sighed and turned to me. "Go and find him. Look for him till you find him, you and King. You don't have to say anything. Just be with him. I got to go to town and see to things."

That was Uncle. He did right, no matter how it might seem to others at the time.

That was a funeral that was well attended, you can be sure. The church wasn't big enough to hold us all; the overflow waited in the grove to follow the coffin across the road to the cemetery, hoping something scandalous would happen.

Uncle met the morning train bringing the coffin and the Second One, whom he dignified by calling Mrs. Salter. He drove her in the Ford up to the church and offered her his arm when he led her aside. Nobody spoke to her except Uncle, certainly not the nervous preacher. Uncle sat with her in the otherwise empty first pew on the left. Aunt and I sat with Aunt May, Lamar, and Johnny-May in the first pew on the right. It was a hot day, and the paper fans were going full blast. Johnny-May had her bloomers on, and I do not lie—they were black for the occasion. She was very quiet, contenting herself with only one flash at me. "How come your uncle is sitting over there with that old son of a bitch?" She whispered it and got no answer from me, because I had none. All through everything Lamar was grim stone, never bothering to try to comfort his mother, who wailed loudly and leaned against Aunt. Aunt put an arm around her and patted her shoulder. The other woman stayed quiet, for which I respected her, but I felt, with Lamar, achingly jealous of Uncle's being with her instead of us.

To the disappointment of the sensation seekers there was no incident. What he could, Uncle had arranged well. After the burying he took the second Mrs. Salter in his car to the next sizable town, fed her in a restaurant (she would have only a chicken sandwich and a cup of coffee, he told Aunt that night), and saw her onto the first train out, the afternoon train that had passed through our own town earlier. He must have timed things carefully.

That night Aunt baked rolls. She didn't do them often, but we always had them after a funeral, I don't know why. To me, eating them came to be associated with funerals. They were more trouble for Aunt, so therefore perhaps her way of showing respect for the dead. The Salters had been invited to have supper with us, but they didn't come; Lamar wouldn't let them. Aunt sent me over with a big bowl of chicken salad, a plate of hot rolls, and half a cake. Aunt May accepted them, but in a whisper, and she didn't ask me to come in.

There was only one sequel to this affair. Oh, Lamar soon forgave Uncle, or seemed to. However he figured it out for himself, he figured it out. And after all, he could reason, Aunt and I had not been party to Uncle's betrayal. Lamar got a regular job at the filling station fixing bicycles as well as working on car engines; he worked afternoons and Saturdays. He made enough to keep them in clothes, and they had the house and the money Aunt May got for sewing. I found out much later that Uncle had had a talk with Aunt May and told her that her errant husband Johnny had left them part of his insurance and that it was enough to feed them forever. He told her that he had arranged with—the woman—that the whole sum would be deposited with the leading grocery store in town for the Salters to draw on as they needed to. Lamar, though suspicious, did not question a thing like insurance, beyond his years and experience to understand. Aunt May accepted her stroke of fortune with eager belief and even began to give herself airs at the store after that, while Uncle paid the bills.

The sequel I mentioned was this. One evening after supper King and I were loitering around the Salter house wanting someone to come out, and finally Lamar did. But he sneaked out, and he went to the tool shed and got a hammer.

"Where you going, Lamar?"

"Nowhere!"

"Lamar! Where you going?" But I could guess from the look on his face where he was going and what he was going to do.

A few weeks after the funeral a truck had arrived in town and been directed to the church and cemetery. The two men in the truck brought a tombstone for Mr. Salter's grave, which they proceeded to erect. Their commission was by direction of the second Mrs. Salter, if she was such. The tombstone had this chiseled on it: "John Ezra Salter. Born, 1890. Died, 1928. Beloved husband of *Isobel* Salter." (The italics are mine.)

"Go home!" Lamar shouted.

I didn't answer, but we didn't go. We followed him, keeping only a short distance behind him up past the burned-out house and the blacksmith shop and the filling station and the Belsers' store and icehouse, up through the quiet town, keeping to the shadows, on up the hill to the cemetery. He found the grave and the tombstone. He struck a match on it and read the inscription for the last time anyone would read it.

He began to cry, and he sounded both angry and bereft as he smashed his hammer again and again on the tombstone. It broke and fell over.

"Lamar!" King kept quiet, but I was crying, too, now. "You can't! It's your father!"

He smashed the broken stone into dust and fragments. When he'd finished, he turned to us, the hammer still in his hand. "Just—leave me alone."

But we wouldn't. We followed him back through the town, past the fireless blacksmith shop, past the ghostly burned-out house, until we were home.

At his door he paused. "Good night," he finally said.

"Good night!" I said as if we'd been out on an evening of fun. King twitched his behind ingratiatingly; he did that because he didn't have much of a tail to wag to express friendship with.

Lamar still hesitated at the door.

"See you tomorrow?" I asked.

"You going swimming? In the morning? Early?"

"Yes."

"I'll be there. Bring King."

"Oh—sure!"

He went into the house to bed and God knows what dreams. King and I went home across the road. I'd never before been so glad I had King to hug while I went to sleep, for it seemed to me Lamar had tried to destroy not only the other woman, but his father, and himself, too.

Chapter

7

NICE WOMEN have sometimes the oddest, the most inexplicable impulse which, thought over, becomes more than impulse: a thing that must be done. Aunt's was to see the electric chair in Milledgeville where the state executions took place. "I don't know why I want to see it," she told Uncle. "I only know I must." She became more explicit. "I don't want to touch it. I don't want to get closer than three feet to it. But I have to see it." Having stated her case, she folded her hands in her lap and waited for him to agree.

Helplessly, he agreed. Trying to buttress illogic with logic, he sought and found a reason to go to Milledgeville, a reason that would make the primary reason for the trip (the viewing of the electric chair) seem secondary, even casually tangential. This was a visit to Aunt's Cousin Madge who lived only five miles outside Milledgeville. It turned out to be a perfect arrangement because Aunt

Madge and I hated each other, and Uncle was determined that I was not to be part of such an expedition anyway.

This is as good a time as any to explain to those who don't know that a boy in a small town in the South in those days was taught to use the word "Aunt" as a courtesy term. Any female in the family, however distantly related, was called Aunt So-and-So if she were adult. In addition, I called Aunt's closest friends, and the mothers of my closest friends, Aunt Belle or Aunt Prudence or Aunt Whatever. I also called the Negro woman who came once a week to wash and iron for us Aunt Jane. I called all Negro women who had much to do with us Aunt. I am aware that this custom was derided as patronizing by people who later concerned themselves with equal rights for Negroes. The fact is that it started out at least as a term of courtesy, and to this day I cannot find it in me to despise it. Similarly, women of equal rank addressed each other as ma'am in polite conversation, in exactly the same way one finds it done in the novels of Trollope and Austen. Far from being servile, it was used to express a certain not unfriendly formality.

Aunt Madge had once come to visit during my tenure with Aunt and Uncle, bringing with her the ugliest brat imaginable, her own, a two-year-old thing. When Aunt Madge insisted that I declare him as beautiful as she proclaimed him, I said honestly that I thought he looked like an old monkey. Aunt Madge slapped me and burst into tears. Aunt told her to keep her hysterical hands off *her* child! Aunt Madge, weeping savagely, said that Aunt had no child of her own! Uncle put them into separate rooms to cool off, and although they made it up on the surface after a couple of hours, neither had yet quite forgiven the other. As for me, it was a good lesson in mother love, best learned sooner than late.

Hence, Uncle's reasoning. They would visit Aunt Madge, whom Aunt was genuinely if who-knew-why fond of, and during the trip they would pay a call on the electric chair. There was no question of taking me along. As full as any other youth of morbid curiosity, I, when I balanced the advantage of seeing the chair against the horror of seeing Aunt Madge and her old monkey, found in myself no gnawing resentment at being left home—especially when I was told that Aunt May had offered to put me and King up for the night Aunt and Uncle would be away.

That is how I happened to be present the night Hubby came into all our lives. It was after supper. Aunt May was in her bedroom sewing a large bunch of pink cloth rosettes to the waist of a wedding dress she'd promised to have ready tomorrow. Johnny-May was with her. Johnny-May was (!) hemming a handkerchief that was to be a present for Aunt to thank her for showing her how to make corn bread and how to tell by feeling the earth in the pot when not to water geraniums. Johnny-May always paid her debts. She and Aunt had just begun to be thick as peanut butter, and Johnny-May was at our house as much as her own.

It started after I funked the recital. Johnny-May, furious at me for having missed my chance to show off, and her fury stoked by having put on bloomers for nothing, appeared in Aunt's kitchen the next morning to announce, "I just want you to know I think he's an old shit-ass for not playing his piece last night." Aunt may have disapproved of the way it was put, but she was in no mood to reject sympathy that morning, and she bent down to give the child a hug and a kiss on the cheek. After that there was no stopping them. Johnny-May became as faithful an attendant on Aunt as Mildred. I never heard Aunt reprove Johnny-May for her language, but gradually Johnny-May's language became an imitation of Aunt's. Aunt never used a word rougher than damn in my presence, and that only once, and to Uncle.

Last light had faded to darkness. Lamar and I, having set his fish lines for the night, gave ourselves the pleasure of a row on the creek, returning just when it got pitch black. We found them in Aunt May's bedroom. Johnny-May was concentrating hard on her hem, keeping the stitches small and tight. The tip of her tongue showed as she held it lightly between her teeth. Lamar teased her a little, not much. They were always pretty good friends, as much as a brother and sister their ages could be. King had picked up a scrap of cloth from the floor and was shaking it without much interest. Lamar had just turned to me and asked me what I wanted to do before bedtime when we were all suddenly struck dumb and alert by a knocking at the back door.

When we'd unfrozen and looked "Who can it be?" at each other, King dropped his scrap and trotted through the house toward the kitchen. Lamar and I followed him. Aunt May and Johnny-May followed us, Aunt May carrying a lamp. In the kitchen we stopped and listened. Presently there was another knock, single, timid. Aunt May, always undependable, screamed. Johnny-May scowled, but I could see her heart beating under her thin dress. King growled low in his throat. Lamar flung the door open, and there stood a shaking, quaking Negro boy about fifteen, all alone. Aunt May almost dropped the lamp, but Johnny-May sensibly took it from her and brought it to the door.

We could see him now. He was barefooted (as were Lamar, Johnny-May, and I); he wore a dirty gray shirt with a ragged collar and faded overalls. His eyes were wide open, and when he tried to smile his teeth were the whitest I have ever seen.

"What'n hell-fire do you want?" Johnny-May demanded.

Lamar pushed her aside. He was taller than the other boy. "Well?"

"I been watching. Not spying, just watching. I seen you two"—his eyes turned to Lamar and then to me—"go off and come back. I didn't want to knock when you were away, for fear of scaring the womenfolk. But I'd seen you earlier eating in the kitchen—and I'm hongry!"

We all relaxed a little. King, who was never wrong about people, set the new tone when he walked up to the boy and twitched his behind in a welcoming way.

"Will he bite?"

"No," I said.

The boy put his hand down and let King smell it properly before chancing a pat to King's head. King turned to us as if to say it was all right.

"Well, come in," Lamar invited.

"Where are you from?" I asked.

No answer.

"When'd you eat last?" This from Aunt May, who could be sensible at times.

"I don't remember." This couldn't be true; anyone hungry remembers when he last ate.

"What's your name?" Johnny-May asked.

"Hubby."

Lamar looked puzzled. "That's not a name. That's just something some women call their husbands."

"I don't know about that," Hubby said. "Hubby's my name."

Johnny-May pushed a chair to the table. "Sit down, Hubby."

Hubby smiled at her. "You a pretty little thing." Johnny-May blushed red and stared at him to see if he were joking.

"Sit down," Lamar said.

Hubby sat and drew his chair up to the table with its cracked blue-and-white-checked oilcloth. It was then we saw how tired he was, by the way he slumped.

Aunt May asked, "Don't you have—people?"

Hubby shook his head.

"We don't have any leftover victuals," Aunt May said tightly.

Johnny-May reached up, took a skillet from its nail on the wall, and banged it down on the stove. "We'll cook. There's still fire. Lamar, go get some stovewood. There's a cold biscuit or two left. We'll fry him some fat back and eggs."

Johnny-May had just made it to six, two weeks before I was due to hit eight, and she was full of her own importance, what with planning to start to school in the fall. Still, I think it was character and pity that made her take charge the way she did. King, always cheery at the idea of people's cooking, wagged his rear approvingly.

Aunt May fell into line and began to slice fat back,

grudgingly thin. Lamar went out for wood. I pulled up another chair and sat by Hubby. King parked himself between us and stared at Hubby in a friendly way.

"He your dog?" Hubby said.

"Yes."

"He looks like a good one."

"Oh, he is." King hassled modestly.

"You feel like one egg or two?" Aunt May said.

"Two," Johnny-May answered for Hubby.

Lamar returned with the wood. The meat began to smoke and sizzle in the skillet. Johnny-May poured milk into a glass and handed it to Hubby. "Drink it. If you're real hungry, it'll keep you from having a gut ache."

"Thank you." Hubby took it and drank it down. Finishing it, he wiped his mouth with the back of his hand and clenched his lips together.

"Go ahead, belch," said Johnny-May.

Laughing, Hubby let go a series of short belches that sounded more like hiccups. "You a sight," he said to her.

Johnny-May giggled, then caught herself and said with stern dignity, "I got bloomers, but I hate to wear 'em."

Hubby nodded seriously.

"I have to start wearing them every day. I'm starting to school. First grade."

Lamar slapped her lightly on the top of her head. "That's where little fools generally start."

"Shit-ass," Johnny-May said to him on her way to the food safe to get cold biscuits and the syrup pitcher. When she deposited these on the table she asked, "Can you read and write?"

"Some," Hubby said.

"Good," Johnny-May said. "You can help me learn. These shit-asses around here are too busy to help me."

It was the first spoken assumption that Hubby might be staying, and it led Aunt May, who was turning the meat, to ask, "Where you going? You say you don't have folks around here."

Hubby looked helpless. "I don't know."

"You must be going somewhere," Aunt May pressed him.

"Just—traveling," Hubby said.

Johnny-May laughed approval of his answer.

Lamar drew up another chair. "Where'd you say you come from?"

Hubby looked frightened. "Oh, I—a long way."

Aunt May took up the meat and put it on a cracked plate they never used except to stand a hot bowl on till it cooled. "You must be going some place if you're passing through here," Aunt May insisted.

"Nowhere particular."

"You can stay with us," Johnny-May offered.

"No, he can't," Aunt May flared, the first time I'd seen her flare at Johnny-May. "We hardly got enough for ourselves. We can't keep another." She broke eggs into the sizzling grease. Drawn by the interesting noise of eggs frying and the smell of meat and hot grease, King shifted his attention from us to the stove.

Lamar shuffled his chair closer. "You sure you've got no folks?"

Hubby nodded, very sure.

"How come you happen to knock at our door?"

"Well." Hubby puckered his brow, thinking, or stalling.

"You see, I was tired and I saw that big house across the road, and I went there thinking the missus would give me something to eat in exchange for some work, but wasn't nobody home. No light. I made a noise and the chickens started a fuss, so I come over here."

"I wouldn't be so sure there's nobody home over there if I were you," Aunt May said, as if she suspected Hubby of being the scout for a gang of robbers. "How do you know they don't just like to sit in the dark waiting for little colored boys?"

"Ah, Mama, hush," Lamar said. Then to Hubby, "You know who lives over there?"

Hubby shook his head; Johnny-May giggled.

Aunt May set down the meat and eggs on the table before Hubby. Then she turned back to the stove and picked up the frying pan.

"Please, ma'am," Hubby said, "if you're going to throw away that grease, just pour it on my plate."

Aunt May, who had not been going to throw it away but was about to pour it into a jar with other grease, hesitated, then brought it to the table and poured it over Hubby's meat and eggs. Hubby broke a biscuit quickly and soaked it in the grease. He began to eat.

Aunt May set down the frying pan, put her hands on her hips, and faced Hubby. "That's a mighty big man lives over there," she said. "Big in this town. He don't like folks sneaking around his place."

"I didn't bother nothing," Hubby said.

"He's got dogs," Aunt May added. "Mean dogs that would as soon eat you as look at you."

Lamar, Johnny-May, and I collapsed with laughter, and

then with tears rolling down our cheeks turned to look at King, who was staring at Hubby, polite but with begging eyes.

"Is he hongry, you reckon?" Hubby said.

"No," Johnny-May said, "his belly's as tight as a tick. Don't you give him a thing."

Hubby went on eating. We watched him quietly, enjoying his enjoyment. When he finished, his plate was clean. He stared at its cracked cleanness, looked up, but not at us, and said, "I thank you."

Johnny-May took the plate away. Hubby shifted his chair back from the table. King licked his chops elaborately, disappointed but resigned. The truth was he hadn't eaten very well that night. Aunt May begrudged food to dogs. She stood now with her arms folded. Her voice falsely bright, she said, "Well, now you've eaten, I expect you'll want to be on your way."

Hubby got up from his chair. "Yes, ma'am. You been kind. I won't forget. I thank you again." He looked at King. "What's his name?"

"King."

He smiled. "So long, King," and reached his hand down to pat King's head. King, as if he had received an invitation, trotted to the door beside Hubby. Hubby made a sudden discovery, looked at me and asked, "Is he the mean dog across the road?"

"Yes," I said. Lamar, Johnny-May, and I laughed with Hubby, and King looked at us all, as pleased as if he'd told a joke.

Hubby opened the door. "Well, so long, everybody." King stood tensely in the doorway. I was almost jealous, feeling that a whistle from Hubby might have got him. King, as if he sensed my thought, looked back at me reassuringly, then again into the darkness. Lamar stepped over King and shaded his eyes, trying to see through darkness.

"Hey, Hubby! Come back here!"

Hubby returned quickly, smiling, hoping. King danced up and down, his nails clicking on the bare wooden floor, as if Hubby'd been gone a month.

"You said you don't know anybody," Lamar said. "If you don't mind sleeping on a pallet on the floor, you can stay here."

"I don't mind!" Hubby said.

"All right, Mama!" He turned to Aunt May. "Make a pallet and put it in my room."

Aunt May looked icicles at Lamar. "He may have bugs."

"No'm, I don't," Hubby said.

Johnny-May said, "You heard Lamar, Mama. If you don't, I will."

Together they went off to find bedding.

Still at the door, Lamar said to Hubby, "If you want to do anything, the outhouse is over there." Hubby shook his head. "Why don't we stand outdoors and breathe deep before we wash our feet?"

The three of us trooped out, King ahead of us. King ran down to the creek's edge to smell things. Lamar closed the door. The lamp from the kitchen cast only a dim light, and our eyes gradually got used to the dark.

"It's dark," Hubby said. "If I closed my eyes and mouth, you couldn't see me, I bet." He giggled.

"Try it," Lamar said. Hubby was quiet. "I can still see

you. There's the Big Dipper. Look. Over there. I got to pee. Let's all go pee on Johnny-May's flower bed."

"No!" Hubby protested.

"She gave it up; she don't care any more; she wants it to finish dying. His aunt"—Lamar nodded toward me in the dark—"she taught Johnny-May how to grow things in pots."

At the word pots we all laughed, and Hubby and I followed Lamar to the flower bed. Then we washed our feet in the creek and went back into the kitchen, King leaving his swamp smells and getting inside just before Lamar closed the door.

"I'm sleepy," Lamar said.

"Me, too," Hubby said.

King yawned.

"I'm not sleepy," I said, "but all right. I don't suppose you have any good storybooks here?"

"No," Lamar said.

At the door of Lamar's room we met Aunt May and Johnny-May coming out. Through the cracked door I saw that the bed was turned down and that a pallet had been laid on the floor beside it.

Aunt May said to me, "I see you washed your feet. Good night." To the world she added, "I'm taking a big butcher knife into my room, so let's don't have any trouble from strangers."

Johnny-May's hands reached out toward Hubby in apology for her mother. One of his reached toward hers, stopped, as if he'd seen the look in Aunt May's eyes. Then he patted her lightly on the head. "Good night, little girl."

Satisfied, Johnny-May giggled and ran off to her mother's room. We went into Lamar's room and undressed. I had a problem. I wanted to sleep on the pallet, because I'd never slept on one. I explained. Hubby and Lamar looked at each other. Lamar said, "I don't mind if you don't." Hubby shook his head negatively, agreeing.

"Come on, King," I said, and flopped down on the pallet on the floor. King flopped down beside me, then got up and turned around four times, finding himself another place. He began to snore before I got used to the sublime discomfort of a floor pallet. Lamar and Hubby got into the real bed and lay on their backs with their fingers laced under their heads.

Lamar said to Hubby, "His uncle will be back tomorrow—at the big house across the road with the *mean* dog?" They laughed. "He'll see you're looked after."

Soon I heard them shift in bed, turning their butts to each other, curling up to sleep. I wondered if Noochy missed us all being at the house. We'd never been away before. King and I would go over first thing in the morning and give him some corn.

Chapter 8

UNCLE had a room in the barn fixed up for Hubby. It would do until winter, and then, if he was still with us, a stove could be put in. Hubby wouldn't tell us where he'd come from. When asked, he'd simply not answer—not look stubborn or sullen—just not answer. Uncle didn't press him. But the first few days he was with us Uncle took him all-over-everywhere, hoping to find people who knew him. He took him to the sawmill and he took him to the farms, but no one had ever seen him before. When he was not off with Uncle, Hubby avoided town, staying close to us and the Salters. He was afraid of something, I knew, but I didn't know what. For a while Uncle had an idea of settling him with a family on one of the farms—he was too young and small for his age to work at the sawmill—but Aunt surprised us by declaring that she needed Hubby to help her.

Aunt had come back from Milledgeville better reconciled with Aunt Madge (*my* name had not been mentioned, she said) and rather quiet about the electric chair. Yes, she'd seen it, she allowed to her lady friends when they asked, and no, she had not touched it; she had gone no closer than *three feet* to it. When pressed about how it looked, she said thoughtfully, not trying to make a joke, "Uncomfortable."

On a place like ours there was always work for another pair of hands and legs. Hubby helped with everything from slopping the hogs to splitting wood for Aunt's cookstove and sawing logs for the fireplaces. He even helped Aunt scrub floors. Sometimes he dried dishes while she washed them. Nobody had to tell or ask Hubby; he'd see something to do and do it. Pretty soon it was as if he'd been with us forever. There was no question of his going, or being sent, away. Uncle took him hunting, and he sometimes, though rarely, helped in one of the harvest fields when they were short of hands.

There was one man in town who hated Uncle. He had no reason; his hatred was as pure as Claggart's for Billy Budd. His name was Toll Weaver. He didn't do anything much except add each year a new one to the passel of towheaded brats he and his wife Ella were raising. He was the one that day at the Caldwells' who'd tried to sic young King on the bull.

The Weavers lived in a shacky place the other side of town. Ella grew a few sweet potatoes and cabbages; Toll helped out at butcherings and took his pay in meat shares; and people gave them clothes now and then to keep from having to look on their nakedness. I've seen some of those children, girls as well as boys, running around in the yard stark naked on occasion when Aunt took a dress or a pair of shoes to Ella Weaver. Toll Weaver wasn't, as people said, worth killing.

His low estate did not, however, keep Toll from having opinions and voicing them. One day when Uncle and I were in the post office getting the mail after traintime Toll sidled over from a bunch of loungers he'd been standing with and said to Uncle, "I hear you took in a nigger stray." Toll was a big and brawny man. If his family ever went hungry, he didn't, from the looks of him. Toll went on. "I hear, too, you take him hunting." Uncle still made no reply. "I don't like to see a nigger with a gun in his hands, it makes me mad."

Uncle looked at him then. "I don't give a goddam what you hear or what you like or don't like. Now get out of my way, Toll, and let me and my boy pass."

Toll stepped aside slowly with a sly, humorless smile.

If this sounds strange to anybody, they don't know the particular kind of democracy that existed in small towns those days. A Toll Weaver had as much to say as Uncle, probably more, being idle and mean-natured.

Hubby and Lamar were friends from the beginning. Being near in age, this was natural. When Hubby couldn't find anything to do at our place, he did things for the Salters, and he and Lamar got to be close. They worked together, and they went off to the woods together. Lamar's gun was in Hubby's hands as much as it was in his own; just as Uncle let Hubby shoot one of his when they were hunting. Hubby and King developed a great sensitivity to each other's thoughts and actions when they were hunting. Hubby always, Uncle said, knew when King *meant* something, and just *what* he meant. As a result, there was a lot of game on our table that fall, and we often had so much we gave some away.

Hubby had a special feeling about Johnny-May, too, and she about him. He never forgot her friendliness on the night of his arrival. He built her a swing with an old tire and a piece of rope in a tree in their back yard, and he was tireless in pushing the swing—Johnny-May laughing with pleasure, Hubby with a big smile on his face.

I saw them a lot—I saw everybody a lot that summer, in town, at the Milly Hole, at parties, and watermelon cuttings. Living with us, being of us, Hubby was always there at our get-togethers. He helped out, but then so did everybody, and he seemed as much a member of the party as anyone else. But we never took him to other people's get-togethers unless he was specifically asked for. Often he was. People would say, "Bring Hubby, too!" when they asked us. It was an easy time.

Hubby kept out of town, though, unless Aunt sent him there on an errand. It was as if he was afraid to meet someone come looking for him.

I went around with Uncle a lot. We liked to be together in the Ford. Sometimes when he'd be frowning over the steering wheel at some work problem or maybe just concentrating on keeping the car in the clay ruts of the road—none of them was paved then—I'd sing—songs I'd learned in school or church. Although proven and guaranteed no piano player, I liked to sing. Usually Uncle and I ignored each other on our rides. Sometimes he'd turn his head and give me a smile or reach over and rough up my hair.

I saw Tussy maybe once or twice a week. Each time was

an occasion for us to gaze at each other moon-eyed and to exchange notes. Once, late in summer, she came to town on the cotton wagon her older brother Jefferson brought to the gin. Hanging around the gin was something the town boys often did. There'd be a line of wagons waiting, and the wait was often so long that people brought lunch baskets. It was something to watch a wagon full of cotton being sucked up the flexible metal suction stack, and something to watch the machine inside that pressed and packed the seeded cotton into bales.

I knew the day Jefferson was coming with a load, so I went on purpose to visit with him during his wait. Sometimes a wagon driver brought his dog along, but instead of riding on the wagon the dog often trotted along under it to get the benefit of its shade.

When I found Jefferson's wagon, I climbed up the wheel spokes and joined him, sitting on the high wooden side. Wagon height was built up to accommodate a heavy load of cotton, planks being added somewhat in the way a leaf can be added to a dining table. I was surprised to find Tussy with Jefferson, and she was shy at first, but I talked along with Jefferson, and pretty soon she picked up a handful of cotton and threw it at me, and I threw a handful at her. After that everybody was relaxed until it got near dinnertime. I saw they had a lunch basket, and thinking they might be getting hungry but shy about starting to eat with me there, I went on home.

I enjoyed being with the farm children, and I liked being at the sawmill. I spent many hours there with King. I liked the rank, sweaty smell of the mill hands, I liked watching them work, I liked the smell of the sawdust, I liked to fall backward in a great pile of it—I liked the food. I often ate with the men—fat back, peas, flour hoecake or corn bread. Sometimes I sat and shelled peas with the cook, a crippled black man who could make fat back taste like chicken. It took a lot of pea shelling to feed that bunch of hungry men.

One day, bored and with nothing to do—there are always such times in a long summer, no matter how busy things seem when you look back—I wandered over to the Salters', King following me. It was a hot afternoon. Everything drooped, the flowers in our yard, the foliage on the trees. It hadn't rained our way for a long time. Every step I made was in black earth the fineness of powder.

Aunt was taking a nap. Uncle was at the sawmill. Lamar was working at the filling station. I didn't know where Hubby was. Aunt May—never a resort for companionship—was probably in her room sewing or poring over a Sears catalogue looking for new ideas for dressmaking. It seemed to me King was the only friend I had in the world still conscious and with enough energy to be with me. I watched him trot across the road with his lazy, body-sideways trot, his tongue sweating, more out of his mouth than in.

When he'd gone around the house to the back yard, he suddenly stopped, standing tense and surprised, lazy no longer. I ran up to him quietly and saw what he was staring at.

Johnny-May was in her swing, but it was not swinging. From the way it looked, she had "let the cat die" long ago, not even bothering to push herself with a toe on the ground. Her arms were around the sides of the tire to hold her in, her cotton head drooped, she was asleep, or almost. Hubby was asleep, sitting on the ground near her. His head rested on his drawn-up knees. But it was the third one of the group that held King's attention and mine. It was a rattlesnake that had come from God knows where, drawn by the heat to cross the yard to the coolness of the creek bank. Hubby was covered by his shirt and overalls, but Johnny-May showed a lot of inviting skin, her bottom out on one side of the tire, her pink legs dangling on the other.

The snake was as big as my arm. He was in the process of coiling himself near Johnny-May. Johnny-May opened her eyes and saw the snake. King growled to warn her, waking Hubby, who lifted his head. Johnny-May opened her mouth, but made no sound. As the snake raised his head and shook his rattling tail, King crept close enough to spring. Hubby sprang, too, caught the child from the swing and held her up high over his head. King caught the snake and bit him almost in two just behind the neck.

Hubby handed Johnny-May to me, took the stirring stick from the washpot, and beat the snake to death, until his head was indistinguishable from the ground he lay on. Johnny-May clung to me. King danced around the snake and Hubby, barking.

Aunt May came to the back door. "What's all the racket?"

"We killed a snake," I said.

"Oh. Well, do keep quiet. I'm trying to take a nap. Over that dress half the night—" The door banged; she was gone. Hubby gave the snake's head a few more bangs for good measure. King twitched his behind, sharing the triumph. Johnny-May lifted her face from my chest, still holding on to me tight. "Don't tell!" she demanded. I set her down on the ground. Hubby picked up the snake with his stick and went to throw it into the creek, King following to see the job done.

"He'd a-killed me," Johnny-May said. "He'd a-killed me sure hadn't it been for King and Hubby." She didn't cry; mainly she seemed to be struck by the wonder of her escape.

When they came back, Johnny-May ran to King—he was almost as big as she was—and gave him a big hug while he covered her face with happy licks. Hubby, looking very serious, washed the stirring stick and put it back into the pot. Then he relaxed some; you could see the tension leave his body.

"Well, that was something, wasn't it?" Johnny-May ran very fast to him, and he caught her up from the ground, letting her twine her arms and legs around his chest. He laughed and set her back on her feet. "What'll we do now to pass the time?" He tagged her lightly on the head as if to assure himself she was still alive and with us. "Johnny-May, you the one to decide."

Johnny-May considered. "Let's make mud pies."

"King can't play that," I protested.

"That's all right. King can watch. He's done enough for one day. You ever think about that dog might want a rest? Now you act nice. I said she was to choose, so we make mud pies."

It was as sharply as I ever heard Hubby speak.

King settled down quite happily, his legs stretched out full before and behind him on the cool, damp earth.

Johnny-May brought a pot of water from the kitchen and a bent spoon to dig with, and we made mud pies. Hubby found a plank, and we set them to cook in the sun. When they began to dry on top, Johnny-May got the spatula from the kitchen and turned them as neatly as if they were pancakes.

We had a good time, and when Lamar got home from the filling station, Johnny-May had got over her shock enough to tell about the snake.

During the next few days she wore her bloomers and went all over town telling everybody who would listen about how Hubby and King saved her from the snake. She was tiresome about it, but people exclaimed properly as if they were interested. Maybe they were. There wasn't much going on in town, and they hadn't heard Johnny-May tell it as often as I had. Only one of them was nasty about it, Toll Weaver. He listened with a couple of others, and when she was done, he said, "Was you wearing your bloomers, like you are now?"

"No! I was home!"

"White girls ought to always keep their bloomers on when nigger boys are about."

Johnny-May flew at him and kicked him as high and as hard as her bare feet could reach. "You're one to talk, the way your brats go naked!"

Toll slapped her, and I took her home. She didn't let herself cry till we were past the blacksmith shop, and even then I think it was because she was just so mad.

I was mad, too, so I told Uncle about it that night. Later, I thought maybe I shouldn't have, but you can't let men like Toll Weaver get away with things; they only get bolder. So I told him, and he made me tell him over again, to get it straight and to make sure I was telling nothing more than the truth.

Uncle didn't talk any all through supper, and Aunt looked at him, worried. Of course, she was as outraged as he was, the way she felt about Johnny-May, but she wasn't going to egg him on to anything by talking it up. After supper Uncle scraped his chair back, took a toothpick from the little glass jar they stood in and started working on his teeth savagely. I sat quiet as Aunt cleared the table. Hubby was off helping pull fodder that day and was sleeping over with the farm family, since they were colored. Uncle slapped his thigh in his decisive way and stood up.

"I'm going to see Toll," he said to Aunt.

She looked frightened. "If you're going, I'm going," she said.

"Just stay and finish up in the kitchen." He tried to laugh, to make light of it. "I'll be back soon. Nothing's going to happen."

"I'm coming with you," she said, and untied her apron.

"If you're going, I'm going!" I said.

To my surprise she made no objection. "We'll all go. King, too."

So off we drove, Uncle not happiest at having us with him, but knowing he was unable to stop Aunt.

We drove first to Toll's house and found out he wasn't there, hadn't been home for supper even. Then Uncle drove through town slowly, looking for him. We found him sitting on the depot steps with a bunch of men. Uncle got out of the car and called him. After a minute Toll ambled over by himself. Aunt and I stayed in the car. King, who always knew trouble, sat beside me on the back seat, rigidly at attention. I held my arm around him, because I knew he'd try to jump out if voices were raised.

Uncle looked at Toll a minute before he said, "I hear you talked filthy and laid your hands on little girl Salter today."

Toll didn't deny it. "She was sassy," he said.

"Maybe she was," Uncle said. "She inclines to be with people who don't respect her. Well, let me tell you something. She's got no daddy, but if I ever hear of you speaking to or going near that child again, I'll kill you."

Toll didn't answer, didn't move. It was dark, so I couldn't see what they were looking at each other, but knowing Uncle, I know it was plenty.

Toll looked toward the car and smiled. "I see you brought your wife and your boy and your dog."

"That cuts nothing," Uncle said. "You got anything to say?"

Toll made no answer.

"Keep away from the girl. If you don't, I'll kill you, and I mean it."

Toll knew he meant it. He didn't bother to go back to his buddies on the steps. They had heard. He walked off into the dark by himself.

Uncle cranked up and drove us home. When he parked beside the artesian well—there was no need to put the car in the barn; it was a clear night—none of us got out right away. We sat there a minute or two. Aunt, who had not spoken at all during the ride home, reached her arm around Uncle and kissed him. It was the first time I'd ever seen that. They were not demonstrative in front of others, including me.

The very next day something happened to put Toll and

Johnny-May and Hubby out of my mind for a while. That summer, dry for us, was rainy in Tussy's part of the county, as I said when I told about jumping off the bridge.

Mosquitoes thrived and with them malaria. Everyone had malaria at one time or another, chills and fever, we called it, nothing much to worry about. It came, you took quinine and listened to your ears ring. After a while it left you weak and you went about your business as usual. I'd had a mild attack earlier that summer after a trip out Tussy's way.

Uncle carried quinine to Tussy, but she got sicker anyway, and died. He came home the middle of one morning, a thing he seldom ever did, told me Tussy had died and that he had bought a gray coffin for her which was on the back seat of the car and did I want to go out there with him after dinner for her funeral.

I rode in the back seat with the coffin on my lap. King sat beside me, quiet and sympathetic, not knowing what had happened, but knowing something bad had.

When Uncle took the coffin inside the house, I stayed in the car with King. I saw them come out, and I got in the front seat and made King sit on the floor at my feet. Tussy's father carried the coffin in his arms. Her mother, sobbing wildly, tried to make grabs at it, but her two older sons managed to control her. They all got into the back seat and we drove to a colored church nearby. The preacher was there, but no one else. It was a busy time on the land, and even Tussy's family would have to work harder the next day for the time they had lost. Crops don't wait for grieving.

The coffin was carried directly to the burying ground

where a grave had been dug earlier that day by Tussy's brother Jefferson. The preacher read the Twenty-third Psalm from a ragged Bible. Tussy's mother began to sing, "Shall We Gather at the River?" and we all joined in. The coffin was set into the grave, and Jefferson began to cover it. It was then Uncle spoke. "Lord, take this dear baby into your heart and into your heaven and let her be happy always."

The grave was filled and ovaled on top. I stayed behind when the others went away. I heard Tussy's mother say to Uncle, "It was a pretty coffin. We thank you. Although I had to cut the bottom and take out some stuffing before Tussy would fit in."

This was to be all?

There was a chinaberry tree nearby. I climbed it, ripped off handfuls of berries and foliage, and went back to the grave. Pressing the berries into the mound, I spelled my last message to Tussy. "I love you." Then I spread the dark-green foliage on top.

From the car Uncle had seen me and waited, but now he called, "Come on, boy."

After we left Tussy's family at their house, I got into the back seat with King, who had been kept in the car during the burying.

The world didn't work right, if Tussy could die. I felt guilty for not having seen her more often, for not visiting her when she was sick. I thought of her the first time she had handed me a note in answer to my first one, running off around the house to be by herself. Dear, sweet Tussy. Watch over me ever and always, all of my days and my nights.

Chapter 9

YOU'D HAVE THOUGHT nobody ever started to school before, the way Johnny-May carried on, but then she always made a lot out of anything that happened to her. Aunt bought a variety of materials, and the three of them—Aunt, Aunt May, and Johnny-May—sat around sewing for weeks. Johnny-May, who'd never before put much stock in bloomers, suddenly went bloomer crazy. She had to have more than anybody. The hours she spent working elastic through the seams of the waist and legs! She had bloomers to match dresses, bloomers that matched other bloomers, and bloomers that matched nothing. Nobody dared lay down a piece of cloth around her for fear she'd have it whipped up into another pair of bloomers before they could stop her.

On the great day Johnny-May was up before the chickens, washed till she sparkled, and dressed in crackling-fresh matching dress and bloomers. Red socks were stretched high over her Sunday shoes, even though it was hot weather and we'd told her most of the children would be going barefoot for another month or more.

When I went over to pick them up, Johnny-May was urging Lamar on desperately, for fear they'd be late and get a whipping. Whipping was more talked about than done at school, but it was done now and then, and Johnny-May was bound that she wasn't going to get one on her first day. When we left their house, King followed us part of the way, even though I had explained to him all about school starting and he'd seemed to take it in. He was still with us when we got to the Belsers', so I asked Mrs. Belser to call him inside and keep him entertained until we got out of sight.

We went on through the roads and the lanes that led to the school, other children appearing ahead of us and behind us from side paths. Lamar and I teased Johnny-May some, but she knew it was just teasing and hardly paid attention.

The first-grade teacher that year was new, a Miss Sally Moultrie, and nobody knew anything about her except that she was from out of town and lived at the boardinghouse—and that she was pretty. That news had gone around town like flood water as soon as she stepped off the train. It was her first teaching job.

Knowing we didn't know her or anything about her, when we got to the school grounds, Johnny-May still had to ask, "Is she mean?"

"We don't know," we both answered.

"Will she let you go to the johnny during classes if you have to?"

Lamar considered. "If you don't ask too often, she will. Now don't go asking just to get out of the schoolroom."

"Where is it?"

Lamar pointed. "That one's for boys, and that other one's for girls."

"What's the difference?" Johnny-May asked suspiciously.

Lamar gave her an answer of sorts. "They put the Sears pages of Bi-lo baby dolls in the girls' place and ads for tents and hatchets in the boys'."

Johnny-May looked gloomily at the two outhouses. "If she don't let me go when I have to go, I'll piss in my bloomers."

Lamar sighed. "Johnny-May, I don't want any trouble from you. You promised to watch your language."

"Oh, I will."

"And don't pick any fights. I don't want to have to fight somebody's big brother for you after school."

"Well," Johnny-May said darkly, "if any stuck-up thing prisses past me and says she's got on better bloomers than mine, I'm going to hit her. Right in the neck where her Adam's apple ought to be." Johnny-May pretended to have received and to be dying from such a blow. Making a horrible face, she went, "Aaaaaaaoooooh!"

"Johnny-May, you mind me, you hear?"

Johnny-May stuck her head up and marched into the school door ahead of us. The first-grade room was right by the door, and Miss Sally Moultrie was standing in the doorway to welcome her pupils. They were right about her being pretty. She had a lot of freckles, but that didn't matter, with her brown eyes and thick auburn hair.

Lamar stepped forward. "I'm Lamar Salter," he said,

"and this is my sister, Johnny-May. She's starting today."

"Hello, Johnny-May." Miss Sally stooped down to shake hands. Johnny-May was either too thrilled or too scared to answer. "What a pretty dress you're wearing!"

Johnny-May held it up in front. "I got bloomers to match."

"Yes, you have," Miss Sally said approvingly and did not laugh. "They're pretty!" She leaned over confidentially. "I hope the rest of my little girls are just half as nice and pretty as you are."

At this obvious, shameless blob of soft butter, Johnny-May's face lost its last trace of belligerence; she smiled a smile that surrendered her very soul. Miss Sally had with one try pinned the tail on the donkey. Even Aunt lost a little luster in Johnny-May's eyes, for a time.

Miss Sally led Johnny-May into the room. "Now, where do you want to sit?" There were only a few children there, trucked in early from farms and gathered shyly at the back. "You're early, so you can choose to sit up front, or back, or anywhere you want to."

"Front," Johnny-May answered promptly.

"Why don't we settle you right in front of my desk?" Miss Sally said, and did.

Johnny-May sat down in the exact middle of her seat, fixed her dress daintily about her, opened the writing tablet she had brought, placed her sharpened pencil beside it, and folded her hands on the tablet, ready for lessons.

Miss Sally came back to the door to wait for other pupils.

Lamar said, "I'm in ninth grade if—well, if she—"

Miss Sally smiled. "Don't worry. She's going to be my favorite." She nodded, meaning it, already decided.

Lamar still couldn't let go. He stuck his head around the

door. "Johnny-May, you be sure to close your eyes when they read from the Bible!"

Johnny-May looked at him with angelic pity, from a far distance.

We didn't see Johnny-May again until morning recess, when we found her in the yard with Miss Sally and the rest of the first grade all in a circle with joined hands, singing and playing, "Go in and out your windows." A fat, freckle-faced boy with his knickers fastened above his knees knelt in front of Johnny-May when they came to the part of the song that goes, "Go kneel before your sweetheart." Lamar and I laughed and went off, he to play ball, I to find that stupid girl who had been so happy at the recital. I found her and gave her a good thwack on the head with the long new pencil I had brought out of class especially.

That afternoon, when Johnny-May joined us and King, who had taken up his old post under the chinaberry tree, Johnny-May announced smugly that she already had a sweetheart, a first-second-and-third best girl friend, three promises of invitations to parties, and that she was teacher's pet. There wasn't anything we could answer.

Aunt worried about Hubby's not going to school, but he said he wouldn't, and he was fifteen and not hers, and there was no one to make him go if he didn't want to. I think the reason he didn't want to go had less to do with not liking school than not wanting his name down on a roll book where he might be traced.

Miss Sally Moultrie landed on the town like a bomb exploding rose petals and frankincense and music. Talk about outsiders finding it hard to be accepted there—such a thing never occurred to her, and it certainly never occurred to anyone else. Inside a week she was town topic number one. They still talk about her in a way they never talked about anybody else. She went everywhere and she knew everybody.

She joined the church and took a Sunday-school class. She went to every dance and party of any kind for miles around. She showed up at the drugstore and the post office at least once a day. If she saw somebody on the street she didn't know she went up to him or her and began to talk, and next time they met they were like old friends. She came to see Aunt and stayed to help her make scuppernong jelly. She helped me feed pears to Noochy. She visited the sawmill with me and King. She went out in Lamar's boat with him and Hubby and Johnny-May. She taught King how to shake hands. She organized a Girl Scout troop. After joining the one church she went off to services now and then at the other because she had so many friends there, she said. She went to see the sick and the well, the good and the ungodly. She even went out to see Ella Weaver, and the second time she went she took her a twelve-pound sack of flour and five pounds of sugar and made her promise to send her oldest girls back to school. She organized a cheerleading team of boys and girls and taught them how to make a lot of noise at exactly the right time to upset any opposing team. She went to a sewing circle, joined the Woman's Club, and made and ate chicken salad and rolls. She was known to accept a bottle of home-brewed beer now and then when it was offered. She made fudge and divinity and passed them around her first-grade classroom while they all learned to read Peter Rabbit.

The thing she had I've never seen in another person in

my life was the quality of making everybody think she was his or her own special friend. She did it honestly; she felt that way about people, and so they felt that way about her. It's no exaggeration to state that every man, woman, and child in that town loved her. She could charm smiles out of the primmest, starchiest old ladies. No child could fear her, or feel that he was much younger than she. No old person could feel boring or useless in her presence. This is not to make her out a Miss Goody Two-shoes. She could fuss and she could cuss, but when she did, people seemed only to like her more. She wasn't even resented by the other schoolteachers. Miss Ernestine Featherstone, the third-grade teacher and therefore mine that year, was referred to generally as "mean old Miss Featherstone," but when we saw her talking to Miss Sally, she might have been an angel of the Lord, so wreathed in benign smiles was she.

Miss Sally's supremacy over all other human creatures being acknowledged—nay, proclaimed—there remained only one question. Who was she to marry?

Marry she must, otherwise we might lose her to another school, another town. She dated everyone who asked her. How she found the time, no one knew. She was free and perfectly open with her kisses, but in a way that made no boy or man feel special. There were, the town decided, only two serious possibilities. They were Elton and Tom Paul Kendrick, bachelor brothers who lived on and worked a big farm a couple of miles out of town. They were known as the Gay One and the Glum One.

Elton was the Gay One, a he-man ladies' man, darkly handsome, tall and muscular, with curly black hair and deep dimples that were said to have been the ruin of more than one girl. He was, in his way, as much a general favorite as Miss Sally was. The only drawback with Elton as a prospective husband for Miss Sally was, everyone agreed, the question of whether or not he was ready to settle down. It was frequently said that if anyone could make him ready, it was Miss Sally. Although he was not good enough for her (no man was) he might do.

On the other hand, there was Tom Paul, the Glum One. He wasn't glum exactly, or only so in contrast to his brother. He *was* serious. He went to parties and dances, but he didn't dance every dance. He seemed as content talking on the side lines with anybody who felt like talking as he was swinging a partner around the floor. He never made jokes, whereas everything his brother Elton said seemed to have some hidden amusing side to it. Tom Paul grew on people; Elton was everybody's good friend the minute they met him. They were both devoted to the farm—good farmers, shrewd businessmen.

It was soon clear that both Kendrick boys were in love with Sally Moultrie. Which would she choose—if either?

It's odd to think now how one girl's romance could so grip an entire town, but so it was. There was no television, radio sets were not yet common, going to movies involved traveling to a town fifteen miles way. The town had only its own drama and dreams to feed on.

The Gay One, Elton, might take Miss Sally to a dance, but if he drank too deeply from the fruit-jar corn in the shadows outside, it was sometimes the Glum One, Tom Paul, who drove her home. If Elton were too hung-over to squire her to church on Sunday morning, Tom Paul did the honors. But that very night it might be Elton, sober and even handsomer for his slightly seedy look, who brought her to evening service.

The brothers, hitherto good friends, fought. Each declared to the other his love for Miss Sally and warned the other off. Both scorned the warning, and they fought hand to hand to a draw. The next Sunday they both escorted Miss Sally to church, in the morning and the evening, both scabbed and bruised about the face and fists.

Miss Sally herself knew by then it would be one or the other, but which one she didn't know for a time. She had no secrets, seemed to feel that, like royalty, whatever she thought or felt belonged to others as much as herself. She liked them both, she admitted, very much. The one she was with was the one she liked the better.

Then she made up her mind. She had decided, she said to an interested group in the drugstore one Saturday morning, that she loved Elton. That night their love was consummated to the almost audible sigh of the whole town. For a week we warmed ourselves on their passion. If this sounds uncomfortably Peeping Tom and vicarious of us, I can only say it didn't seem so then. There was an open heartiness about the whole thing that made it seem all right.

Elton took Miss Sally out somewhere in his car every night. He even visited her during play recesses during the day and joined the delighted first-graders in their game of "In and out your windows." When he was It, and they sang the part, "Go kneel before your sweetheart," he went around the inner ring, comically looking as if he was studying it over and trying to make up his mind. Then he almost kneeled before Miss Sally before running over and kneeling in front of Johnny-May, who he knew was her pet. Everybody whooped, and Lamar and I almost had to take an ax to Johnny-May that afternoon, she was so proud and boastful. Every day after school Elton waited for Miss Sally in his car, and off they rode. Everybody waited for the day to be announced.

Then lo and behold, exactly a week after the whole thing started, Miss Sally put an end to it. She told Elton, and she told everybody else that she was sorry; she admitted her mistake, but she had been wrong. It wasn't Elton she loved at all, except as a brother maybe; it was Tom Paul. Well! It was a little late for changing her mind, everybody thought, but Miss Sally could do anything, it seemed. Elton was stunned and disbelieving at his rejection. He didn't take it seriously at first, and when he did, he went out with a different girl every night. That town's never known, before or since, so many girls that got pregnant because one other girl had a change of heart.

We waited for Tom Paul to come forward and claim his prize, but he did no such thing. When he'd been rejected in favor of his brother, he'd taken it hard, not shown his face in town or at a single dance or party. He stuck to farming, and when anybody saw him, as they did when he started coming back into town again, they didn't dare mention Miss Sally to him. Nobody made free with Tom Paul.

So Miss Sally settled down to wait for Tom Paul. She had dates, she went around with other men and boys, but everybody knew she wasn't serious about them. When it got near Christmas she took a whole lot of children into the woods one Saturday to cut holly and Christmas trees, making a party out of it.

After Christmas it became obvious that Miss Sally was pregnant. She'd known all along, but it was one thing she kept to herself until others could see it for themselves. Then, when it was mentioned, she talked about it easily. Yes, she was going to have a baby, and of course it was Elton's. He went to see her and told her she had to marry him now. She told him if he was in a marrying mood, he could take his pick of any of those other girls who would begin to show pretty soon. She, she told him, would wait for Tom Paul to come for her. She knew he loved her, she said, and she loved him, so it would be foolish to marry anybody else.

The remarkable thing was that nobody blamed Miss Sally. She was as popular as ever. She had been mistaken in her first judgment—well, that could happen to anybody. There was never any real question of dismissing her from her job at school, and she did not offer to leave.

Miss Sally was not the first young unmarried teacher to find herself pregnant, but the ones before her had been married off pretty quickly and quietly when their transgressions became known. Miss Sally said, perfectly fairly, that she was just as good a teacher as she'd been before, and besides she liked the town, so why should she leave it? All of her first-grade class, not just Johnny-May, worshiped her, and she them. She got bigger and bigger, and when she was too big to play games with the children, she sat on the sides and watched them, laughing and participating almost as much as she had before. Johnny-May often sat beside her, giving up the game for her company, frequently sewing at something for Miss Sally's baby. When the school principal got worried and went for advice to Miss Sally's preacher, he just threw up his hands and said he didn't know, for once he couldn't advise.

Things went on like that through the spring. Miss Sally and Tom Paul never met face to face. If they were at the same party, he stayed on the other side of it away from her. This was a new thing for the town. They felt something had to happen and soon, before the baby came, but nobody seemed to have a suggestion. Several boys offered themselves as alternate husbands, but Miss Sally just thanked them and said she couldn't. Just as she'd taken us into the woods for holly and trees, she took us when spring came into the woods to pick violets. She gave an Easter Egg Hunt in the grove of churches, and everybody came except the Kendrick boys.

When the end of term neared, Miss Sally announced that she would leave us after the last day of school if Tom Paul had not asked her to marry him. A delegation went to Uncle and talked it over. That afternoon he drove out to see Tom Paul, taking Johnny-May with him. I don't know what kind of case they put to him. Neither Johnny-May nor Uncle would talk about it, but they came back looking not very satisfied.

Then on the very last day of school, after report cards had been passed out (Johnny-May got all A's, and wasn't she something to deal with), we were all standing around the school grounds saying our good-bys. Although we'd see each other almost as much during the summer, it was a ritual we observed. Up drove Tom Paul in his car. If he'd ever deserved the name of the Glum One, he did now. He came over to Miss Sally, who was standing laughing with Miss Featherstone and looking big as a circus tent. He took her by the arm and said, "Sally, we're going to get married. Come on." He ought to have known better.

She pulled her arm away and said, "No. You have to ask me."

He hesitated. "I'm asking you."

"Well, say it."

"Come on, Sally, let's get married." He actually ground his teeth, and certainly looked more like a murderer than a lover.

"I won't unless you say it right."

He looked at her as if he could kill her. What agonies of embarrassment she was making him suffer! But then, he *had* made her wait. "Sally, I love you. Will you marry me?"

"Yes, Tom Paul. I love you, too."

"Well, come on. We can drive over to Swainsboro and be married by nightfall—"

"No, Tom Paul. I want a church wedding. I'm not going to run and hide from God and the people here I love."

Nor did she. She had no close relations; she was an orphan like me. She stayed on at the boardinghouse until things could be properly arranged. When Elton heard what had happened, he lit out for California where he bought an orange grove after he'd arranged by mail to sell out his share of the farm to Tom Paul. It was told later he'd married and settled right down, as though he'd learned his lesson, and was a model husband and father.

Miss Sally brought her wedding-dress material to Aunt

May, who insisted on making it up for nothing. Miss Sally had decided on all white except for a little bunch of pink rosettes at the waist, as if in honest admission of the large swell there. She was a fat but a beautiful bride. Uncle gave her away. Aunt was matron of honor. The only other attendant was Johnny-May, all dressed in pink and looking like Christmas had come, she was so pleased with everything. She had got up before daybreak to gather flowers and pull off their petals into her beribboned basket. She scattered them so daintily down the aisle it set Lamar and me to crying, it was so beautiful.

After the wedding there was ice cream and cake at our house, and Miss Sally made over King a lot because he hadn't been allowed to come to the wedding. Tom Paul took her right off to his farm. There was no wedding trip. Four days later Miss Sally had a baby girl whom she named for Johnny-May. Elton never came back, and we got over missing him. Miss Sally is in her late fifties now, going gray but still laughing and girlish, even after seven more children. Everybody loves her as much as they always did, and every birthday Johnny-May sends her namesake a present. Tom Paul loosened up a whole lot after he got married. He even tells jokes now and then, but not about the past.

Chapter 10

To GO BACK.

Everything that winter was not concerned with Miss Sally.

All summer and fall as I watched Noochy grow up and fill out, a cloud grew in my mind, because I knew he was to be killed that winter. Uncle had been fair with me. He explained to me that first and foremost he was a farming man. Some animals, cats and dogs, were pets in addition to earning their way by keeping the rats down (Tom and presumably Mildred), by helping him hunt, and acting as general protection of property (King). The other animals, chickens and pigs and cows, were raised to provide us with food. Sooner or later they would do this, so it was best not to let ourselves get too fond of a particular one.

I told him I understood, and I thought I did. But six months or a year from now doesn't mean anything to a boy. It seems forever away. Having explained it to me and made sure I understood, he let me and Noochy alone. He was a busy man, he had a lot of other things to think about; and of course he knew he couldn't stop my making a pet of Noochy anyway. So Noochy and I unwisely kept on the way we were going. He wasn't as close to me as King, or even Tom. He didn't have any tricks or talents. All he did was recognize me, grunt at me in a special way, and love me, as I loved him, because we'd picked each other out. However, he wasn't mine, and I knew it as well as anybody. I began to realize with horror that my very friendship with Noochy—feeding him pears and other extras the other hogs didn't get—made him one of the readicst for the table.

Uncle generally killed his own hogs twice a winter, the first bunch when the weather had stayed cold a few weeks, late November or early December, the second bunch along in late January. The weather turned cold in November and stayed cold. There was frequently ice on top of the milk pitcher in the morning, a heavy frost over the fields, and as the weather stayed cold, icicles hung from the windmill where water dripped down from the tank.

The winter before, my first with Uncle and Aunt, the whole thing had been exciting—gruesome, but still something wonderful, my first hog killing. Everybody was up long before daylight, Aunt in the kitchen frying great platters of fat back and eggs to feed the extra hired help who were even then stamping around in the yard, rubbing their hands, exhaling steam, making fires around pots of water the hogs would be scalded in to make it easier to scrape off their hair.

They were killed in two ways. A great trough of slops would be poured, and while they ate, some of the hogs would be shot through the head and others would be hit on the head with the blunt end of heavy axes. The latter way was preferred, I believe, because it made for cleaner dressing of the meat—no shot to be picked out. Both ways were brutal; killing is killing.

The year before I hadn't seen the killing. Aunt had kept me in the kitchen after the others had eaten their breakfasts, stuffing me with extra food until it was nearly time to send me off to school. I had only seen them dipping and scraping the hogs and hanging them up by their hind legs so that they would bleed cleanly. I had gone off to school, and when I returned there were the fascinating activities to watch of sausage making and souse making. The great coils of sausage and the hams were hung in the smokehouse to cure. For days after there were fresh backbone and roasting pork. There were also chitterlings and blood pudding, which I refused to touch. And the crisp, freshly made cracklings to eat with the fingers or in bread. The thing was like a big jolly working party, with jokes and laughing, and all the extra help going away when it was over with fresh meat for their families. Lamar had blown up two of the clean bladders and let Johnny-May and me punch them into the air like balloons, but they wouldn't stay blown up for long.

Noochy in mind, I did not think of it as a happy party this year. Then I had what I thought at first was a fine idea, indeed a solution to my problem. I went at once to Uncle and told him. We wouldn't kill Noochy at all! We'd keep him instead for stud! (One or two of the boars were kept over each year for the purpose.)

Uncle looked at me frowning, but with feeling in his

eyes. Finally he said, "No, boy. Noochy isn't good enough."

"What do you mean, Uncle? Noochy's the best!"

"No, boy, he is not. He hasn't got the proper build. He'd bring down my whole breed, and I can't have that."

I knew very well what he meant, as I had really known, against hope, that he wouldn't accept my idea. Noochy had been the runt of his litter before I made a pet of him. Although he had got stout with my indulgences, he didn't have the height and strong frame of his brothers. He'd been the runt, even when grown, and runts are always killed.

I didn't give up. "Uncle, seeing he's not quite as big as the others, not as tall, I mean, but he's fat—couldn't we save him for a while? Until the next time?"

Uncle looked at me, considering. Finally he shook his head. "It won't be any easier for you, or for Noochy, if we put it off. It'll be harder for you, because you'll worry yourself until it happens. Don't go looking for trouble. It'll find you soon enough."

I knew I had lost, and trying not to cry, I cried. "One hog doesn't mean anything to us, Uncle! Can't you give him to me? I'll take care of him. He'll just be my special hog."

Uncle looked pained, but he didn't change his mind. I begged Aunt to intercede, but she would not. She knew she could not. "No," she said. "I was wrong before."

Hubby was to help with the killing, and he was looking forward to it. I begged him as a special favor to kill Noochy himself. We went to Uncle together.

"All right," he said to Hubby. "You can use my gun."

The day before it was to be, I took Hubby aside, and

together we went down to see Noochy. We made over him, and I scratched his back with a hard stick just as long as he could stand it, and finally, bored with us, he trotted off to be with the other hogs. Hubby and I sat on the top of the fence and watched him awhile. "Promise me, Hubby," I said, "you'll do it just as—?" There was no need for me to finish.

"He won't know a thing," Hubby said. "And I'll pray for him when I do it." I knew Hubby meant what he said.

I was up early next morning, but for once didn't feel like eating. Aunt made me drink a glass of milk and eat a piece of leftover chocolate pie before she let me go over to the Salters'. Syrup beads had formed on the egg meringue, and I ate just the chocolate part underneath. I got to the Salters' long before they were ready to go to school, and I had a cup of coffee with them while they ate breakfast. They knew why I was there so early, and were kind in an offhand way. King had not followed me. He was much too excited by all that was going on at our place.

Lamar and Johnny-May and I trooped off together, trying to laugh and cut up as usual, but none of us had our hearts in it. After all, they knew Noochy, too. We got to the school grounds before anyone else; there was not even a light at the Belsers' when we passed; and we found the school doors still locked.

Lamar allowed himself only one reference to the day's event, and that was when Johnny-May, shaking with the cold, ran off up the lane hard as she could tear, to get warm. "One thing I don't like. You told me Hubby promised to do it and your Uncle said all right. Well, then he went and hired Toll Weaver for the day, because he knew Toll's family needed meat. Your uncle's too good sometimes for his own good. Toll's had his eye on Hubby ever since the snake and Johnny-May, and we both know how he hates to see a colored boy pull the trigger of a gun, even if it's only at—a hog. And he won't know the reason Hubby's let do it."

Lamar was right. Toll Weaver took his pay in a generous amount of meat, but he went around saying, "You see how he let that nigger boy pull a trigger on his own hog?" Nobody listened to Toll much, except his cronies, but they all heard him.

When I went home that afternoon, late as I could make it—I almost wished I had a lesson with Miss Spiers—almost everybody was gone, just Uncle and Aunt and a couple of the regulars. Aunt made occasion to say to me they'd given all of Noochy away, and I wasn't to think when I ate that I was eating any of Noochy. She may have been telling the truth; she may not have. If she was not, her lie allowed me after a few days of silently refusing all pork, with a shake of my head, to eat it again. Even so I felt like a cannibal. But appetite and greed can be stronger than love and memory. In some ways I suppose we are all cannibals.

Chapter 11

IT WAS King's love of being with people that almost proved his undoing. I've said how he liked to hang around with the loafers in the barbershop or on the depot steps. Well, idle men, bored and wanting even a few minutes' excitement, will sic a friendly dog on any creature that passes. They tried King on a couple of stray cats. When they dropped the cats on him, naturally he attacked them and killed them. That caused no fuss. Nobody complained when a cat nobody knew turned up corpse-stiff in the middle of the road until somebody threw it into a ditch or, for a joke, onto the back of a passing wagon.

King wouldn't have been hanging around with them so much if I hadn't been in school and Hubby hadn't been shy of town, as I told Aunt and Uncle. But he was with them a lot, and so the inevitable happened. He killed *Somebody's* cat when he was told to "sic him." It was a perfectly ordinary store mouser, from Mr. Palmer's store.

To my knowledge nobody had even bothered to stoop down and give that cat a pat or a kind word, but when King killed him, suddenly *he* was a bad dog, he had tasted blood, he should be tied up. If he kept on like that, it was said, people would set out poison for him.

The way it happened, I was told, was this. King was sitting with them on the depot steps, listening to them tell their dull old dirty stories for the hundredth time, when the cat (he had no name until his death when he was promptly called Tom) decided to leave Mr. Palmer's store for a stroll. He sashayed across the railroad tracks, paused to look at the dog and the men there—he wasn't afraid of King; they'd seen each other many times before—when Toll Weaver got his idea.

Toll picked the cat up, slapped him until the cat was scared and mad, then dropped him on top of King and said, "Sic him!" The cat landed on King's back full of fight, and King killed him. The only innocent party, it seemed, was Toll. He hadn't meant anything, was just trying to have a little fun.

But when the crowd of men scattered and Mr. Palmer came running at the noise, there was only King and the dead cat. A lot of tales were told before the true one, and that not by Toll, but by one of his more innocent fellow loafers. By then it didn't matter. King's name might have been King Herod.

Mr. Palmer complained to Uncle who said he was sorry, and offered him the pick of Mildred's next litter—indeed, all of it, if that would make amends. But Mr. Palmer went away unmollified. His cat of no consequence was a martyr to the savagery of my dog.

After that, when Aunt went into town, which she did every day or two, she was approached by various ladies at the drugstore and post office and asked what she was going to do about King. They were generally ladies who had pet pussies that did occasionally stroll from home, and they wanted to be assured that their favored ones would be safe from the bad dog. Aunt said she didn't know what she'd do, but she'd try to think of something. One repeated suggestion she refused. She would not tie King up. She knew good and well he'd been egged on to doing what he'd done, and she wasn't about to chain him when the fault lay with those idle men.

I heard what happened only when she told Uncle. Busy though she was, she began to keep a watch on King. One day, missing him suddenly when he'd been at her heels a few minutes before, she went to the front door. Sure enough, there he was, almost out of sight, trotting off toward town and the company of men.

She changed her shoes quickly and threw a shawl around herself and followed him. He was out of sight, but she knew where he'd be. When she got to town she spied him across the railroad tracks, sitting at the feet of the men on the steps. She went about her business as if it were ordinary, into the drugstore for some bobby pins and Sal Hepatica. Then she ordered a Coca-Cola at the fountain, with a cherry and lots of ice, as she always did, and sat on a counter stool, so she could watch through the window.

She hadn't been there five minutes, she said, just gossiping lightly with Mr. Blake, the druggist, when she saw Toll Weaver leave the bunch of men on the steps and go over to the little house across the road which served as the meeting place for the Woman's Club. Their cat was sitting on the porch on a chair in the sun, minding his own business. Toll picked him up and carried him back to the depot steps. The other men scattered but stayed near enough to watch, fearful of and wanting trouble.

Aunt left the drugstore like a streak of lightning. She ran across the tracks and got there just as Toll dropped the cat on King's back. She shouted King's name, grabbed up the cat, and threw it across the road. The cat, needing no encouragement, climbed to the roof and sat looking down at the scene that ensued. Aunt grabbed King by a hind leg, threw him over on his back, and began to slap him about his muzzle. He never resisted Aunt; he knew that when she got mad at him, she had a reason, even if he didn't understand it. He lay there and took it. Then she lectured him, shaking her fist in his face, telling him that if he ever touched another cat, she—well, she didn't know what would happen to him, it would be so awful. She finished the first part of her scolding, and King got to his feet, looking thoroughly ashamed and apologetic. He tried to give a friendly shake of his behind, but she kicked him on it and told him to go home and stay there. He went.

Then she looked around for Toll, and found him. The other men drifted closer. This wasn't the excitement they had expected, but it was all the better for that. She went up to Toll, shook her fist in his face, and gave him a piece of her mind. She felt, she told Toll, like tearing him limb from limb. She also felt, she said, that she could have at the time, big as he was. But she contented herself with saying he'd be doing more good looking after his family than sitting around with worthless (a shake of her fist to them) men and teasing dogs into mischief. After which she went back to the drugstore, finished her Coca-Cola, chewing up all the ice good and hard to work off her rage, claimed her bobby pins and Sal Hepatica, and went home.

But that was not the end of King and the loungers. Oh, he stayed close to home for a few days, but when Aunt got so sure of him she didn't watch him closely any more, he went off to them. Toll wanted to get at us, and he didn't scorn what even he must have thought a measly way.

Soon after, Aunt sent Hubby to town on an errand. It was a washday, and Aunt Jane was there, acting a little grumpy. She and Aunt had been boiling and beating the dirt out of clothes all morning, Aunt nipping into the house now and again to see how her dinner was going, before she discovered that Aunt Jane's crossness was due to the fact that she'd run out of snuff. Hubby was dispatched to town to get her a tin of Yellow Buttercup and a jar of black Bruton, with the red-not-the-white label. I was often sent off to buy them for her myself and with the same red-not-the-white warning.

I loved watching Aunt Jane mix the two snuffs together on a newspaper laid out on a table. She'd blend them carefully, and then pack them back into the jar and tin they'd come in, holding jar and tin upside down and going over the snuff on the newspaper until it was all packed in. Sometimes on washday Aunt had a dip with her to be sociable, but she was not a regular dipper. She said if she did it too often it made her dizzy, just as smoking a cigarette did. She wasn't a smoker either, although now and then she'd take one with Uncle after supper.

Nor was Aunt a drinker, but when she baked her fruitcakes in the early winter, she always had Uncle bring her some liquor to pour over them. She wrapped the cakes in old clean sheeting and packed them into round wooden cheeseboxes, which she'd have Mr. Palmer save for her. Every week or so she'd open the boxes, unwrap the cakes, pressing them lightly on the sides with her thumbs to find out how dry or moist they were. If they were dry, they had a little more whisky poured over them. Once in a great while, usually around Christmas when we had friends in, she'd take a drink with them to be jolly. Uncle knew not to give her much. A few sips made her happy, but if she took any more she was likely to get to thinking about her little girl, dead and buried in the cemetery, and she'd cry. That grief and regret never left her; she carried them always just beneath whatever her surface mood happened to be.

But to get back to Hubby. Aunt gave him the proper change for the snuff and a nickel over to buy him some candy for his trouble, and off he went, followed by King. While he was in the store, King went sniffing off to the barbershop. He loved the smell of hair oil and talcum powder and bay rum.

When Hubby finished the snuff transaction, he went looking for King. He found him in the barbershop with that bunch of men, lined up in the waiting chairs, as if they were waiting their turn for the scissors and the clippers, although few of them had a shop haircut from one season to the next. They were sitting laughing, all except Toll Weaver, who had brought in the cat from the bank next door. The barber was nervous. Everybody knew that cat. He was a big ginger, and his name was Money. This wasn't like playing with strays or even throwing Mr. Palmer's cat to the sacrifice. (He had, since his loss, accepted two of Mildred's male kittens, figuring maybe that two would be safer than one.)

Hubby went right up to Toll. They knew who each other was, although they'd never said a word directly either way. Hubby said, "Please, Mr. Weaver, don't start mischief with King and that cat!"

Toll said, "I'm used to having nigger boys call me Mister Toll instead of Mister Weaver. It's more respectful."

"Please, Mister Toll! You'll get us all in trouble if King kills another cat—and you know he will if you tell him to." King trotted over to Hubby. "That's right, King, you come on with me."

Toll got between Hubby and the door. "Who's *us all?*"

"Me and King and—*you* know us all!"

"You mean you one of the family. Related, maybe?"

"That ain't what I mean, you *know!*"

Toll had the cat. Money yowled and lashed his tail against Toll's rough handling, but King wasn't to know that. King growled, and Hubby bent to quiet him. As King turned to Hubby, Toll kicked King. King rounded on Toll, growling seriously now, not at the cat but at Toll. Toll let the cat jump out of his arms and run out of the barbershop unmolested. King still growled, and Hubby held onto him. Toll wiped his mouth with the back of his hand and spat hard into a spittoon. He looked as if he wanted to hit Hubby, but King's growling held him off. He was scared of King; it showed on his face, Hubby said. He sauntered over to the men. "You see that nigger? You see that dog? Trying to attack me. You're my witness. Have I done anything?"

He turned to Hubby. "Get your dog and your black ass

out of here, and go tell them Toll Weaver ain't going to put up with sass from their dogs or their niggers from now on."

With the help of the barber Hubby got King out of the shop, and the barber closed the door on them.

There wasn't anything Uncle could do. When he heard what had happened, he clenched his hands together and wanted to go fight Toll. But Toll had not actually laid a hand on Hubby, and although he had kicked King, King had threatened him. He decided he had to keep quiet for the time being. But he knew another time was ahead waiting, when it was going to be between him and Toll.

Hubby was disappointed that Uncle didn't go right up and have it out with Toll, but he took it on himself after that to look after King when I was in school. We asked the Belsers to keep an eye out for King and turn him back if they saw him going into town alone. He knew them and would generally mind them. The only time King was allowed to go past the Belsers' was when hc came to meet me and Lamar and Johnny-May after school, and Hubby always came with him.

Chapter 12

I LEARNED to recite the names of all the books in the Bible that winter, in proper order, Old Testament and New. To reward me Uncle gave me a dollar. Not holding with churchgoing for himself, he nevertheless went along with it for women and children. I wanted to follow his example, but I was made to follow Aunt's.

It wasn't all bad. I liked the singing, and every now and then there was a party. But I could never get it through my head that there was much good in it. People whose souls and chance of heaven I wouldn't give you a nickel for would sit there in the house of God, bold as bishops. Then when it was over they'd go off and act just as dirty as they always had.

When I got that dollar, Aunt suggested that the truly Christian thing to do with it was put it in the collection plate next Sunday. But that didn't seem to me such a good idea. Uncle always gave me a dime to put in the collection plate, which seemed to me quite enough for the Lord, considering His riches. I told Aunt that putting a dollar in would look like showing off. I spent some of it on sparklers and firecrackers at Christmastime, and some of it I spent learning to smoke. Lamar bought me a pack of cigarettes, because they'd sell them to him but not to me. He and Hubby and I went off to the woods in his boat together and smoked some of them. They didn't make us sick; we liked the floating feeling they gave us; it seemed to go with being in the boat. Before, all we'd had to smoke was the leaves of a weed called rabbit tobacco we rolled in newspaper strips.

Next Sunday I had some cigarettes left, so, boldly, feeling like a cloven-footed, fork-tailed sinner, I took them with me to Sunday school. I didn't have anything in mind, just vague mischief. Feeling them in my pocket was almost adventure enough.

After Sunday school there was always a little wait before the sermon, and the boys usually killed this time by going deeper into the grove back of the churches where there was a pond covered with lily pads and scum. Lamar, a couple of other boys, and I went around there, and I pulled out my cigarettes and lit up. Then I gave one to Lamar, and he lit up. The other boys watched us admiringly and begged for the ducks. I told them there wouldn't be any, that we smoked them right down to the end; but not to be mean I offered them whole ones which they took eagerly.

I'd learned that having been a city boy carried a certain glamour. After they'd accepted me as more or less one of themselves, they still considered me an authority on wicked city ways. I did nothing to discourage this view, although God knows there was nothing I could have taught those country boys. Well, one of them got sick, much to the disgust of the other three of us, and after he threw up he was still sick when the last bell for church sounded. He started to cry, but he came along with us, and when he got into church he told his mama, because he was scared. She took him out, pausing to tell Aunt in a whisper exactly what had happened and who was responsible.

Aunt sat through the sermon, but she was pretty strained, and her voice cracked when she sang. So did mine. I knew I was in for something. After the sermon she hardly paused on the steps to answer greetings; she hustled me right off to the car Uncle had brought to meet us. Looking scared, Lamar refused a ride, and he and Johnny-May went off with a group of children. Aunt didn't say anything in the car, but when we were inside the house she had plenty to say. Uncle just stood amazed as she shook me and told me I had disgraced her. She sent me off to my room to *stay* there until she had dinner on the table and had Discussed the Situation with Uncle. Furthermore, I was not to have dessert. It happened to be one of my favorites that day, cocoanut cake made with fresh cocoanut which I had helped her grate the day before.

As soon as I was out of sight, but not out of earshot, her voice rose so high, she explained the whole thing to Uncle, or rather, since she didn't have many facts in hand, she repeated what she knew. She suggested that it would be none too good for me if he gave me a whipping immediately after dinner. But he wouldn't take it seriously. I think he tried to, but suddenly, in spite of her fuming, I heard him laughing. He said, "You see what comes of giving him a dollar for learning the books of the Bible?"

She went off to the kitchen, put out with both of us, and

we were snubbed all during dinner. He and I went for a walk with King, while Aunt lay down to quiet her nerves. When we came back, she was herself again and asked if we wanted a piece of cake to tide us over till supper.

It seems to me now that all three of us, Lamar, Hubby, and I, got the notion about the same time, that of camping in the woods. It grew out of something we'd taken to doing in the fall. Unlike me, Lamar and Hubby liked to fish from the boat. The creek was full of little islands. We'd landed on all of them at one time or another to explore. Not that there was anything to explore beyond a growth of palmetto, the same old trees we knew, and occasionally a piece of trash that had washed up on the bank. But an island satisfies in a boy the need to make himself separate and independent of the adult world. And camping is early evidence of his wanting to break away from family, be his own man.

We took to carrying a skillet and some lard and meal with us. Frequently, after they'd caught fish, we landed on an island with King, built a fire, and cooked. We scaled the fish and washed them in the creek, fried them and thin hoecakes of corn bread in the skillet. It was a greasy meal, but we liked it, and it was a fine feeling to sit on the sand around the dead fire after we'd eaten. King got only corn bread, because we didn't want any fish bones choking him.

As winter went on, we thought of those times and longed for spring and summer. The idea came to buy a tent and camp out, then—why not, we decided, build a permanent shelter where we could leave things, instead of having to carry them back and forth? I broached the idea of a tent to Uncle. He said wait till summer; he'd see.

Summer was forever away, too long to wait, and the urge

didn't wait. We studied every tent and knife and hatchet in the Sears catalogue. We made lists of what we'd need, even to small things like nails and matches and salt. We knew to the penny what each and all would cost. At first we thought of buying things gradually and putting them aside to use later. But none of us had much spending money, and it was easier to buy a candy bar or a bag of parched peanuts for now than it was to buy a box of matches or salt for later.

In January, after Uncle's second hog killing, the weather turned warm, as it sometimes does that month with a false spring. It was warm enough at night to roam around. Once we gathered a bunch of boys together and went up to the teachers' boardinghouse after supper to serenade Miss Sally. It was about the time everybody decided she was going to have a baby, and she was waiting for Tom Paul to come to her, and we thought she needed cheering up. We sang "Let Me Call You Sweetheart" and "Santa Lucia" and then hollered for her to come out on the porch. She did, and she cried a little, she was so pleased. So to make her laugh again, we sang a song very popular in town just then. "Yes, Sir, That's My Baby." She laughed a lot and told us she loved us all and went back inside.

None of us knew then the line "If Winter comes, can Spring be far behind?" but if we had, we'd have answered hell yes. We were sick of winter, of books and school and all indoor things. Lamar and I started working on Uncle about letting us camp in the woods overnight. He said it was damp and might turn cold suddenly and we might get sick. We persuaded him to take us in his car to a dry woods Hubby had discovered about three miles from town, past the cotton gin and the colored church, past farms where, when you turned off the main road, there was just one field and then woodland.

It was a beautiful, clear, warm day, and we knew where we were leading him. King frolicked around barking over the dry-leafed floor of the woods after we left the car, having himself a good time but also, it seemed to us, trying to help us bring Uncle around to our plan.

He was cheerful, and maybe he remembered a time in his own boyhood when he wanted to do the same thing. What decided him was our showing him an abandoned one-room house we had found on an earlier trip, standing right there in the woods. It actually had a fireplace and chimney, and it looked fairly clean. Uncle had us gather some wood and build a fire to see if the chimney drew. It worked fine. We knew it would; we had tried it. He went around testing the three windows to see if the shutters closed snugly—they had no glass, of course. They did. He gave in, laughing.

"Well, if the weather holds, and if the womenfolk don't object too strongly, maybe you can come out Saturday and stay over Saturday night, coming home Sunday."

That was, we exclaimed, just what we wanted to do.

Uncle said, "You think it's a good idea, King?" King jumped up and down, making it clear in no uncertain terms he thought it a fine plan. Uncle turned to us. "You sure you won't get scared at night?"

"Scared!" Lamar jeered.

"I'll say not!" I promised stoutly.

Lamar and I pounded each other on back and shoulders in a human equivalent of young roosters crowing.

The weather remained good. Aunt, who left the mystery of growing boys pretty much to Uncle, unless I was sick, agreed. The only demur was from Johnny-May, who thought we were hateful not to want to take her along. Aunt promised her the Saturday afternoon in the drugstore, where she was to have her choice of any two cold drinks and a small bottle of Coty's toilet water. So that hushed *her*. Hubby and King were to go with us, of course. I knew Uncle was giving Hubby some firm instructions, but I knew, too, that when we got Hubby off with us, he'd see things our way.

Lamar and I insisted on walking out, like real campers, with croker sacks on our backs. Hubby, wiser from his experience on the road, drove out with Uncle early Saturday morning with quilts and sheets to make pallets and a bundle of fat-lighter wood, in case we had trouble making a fire. In our sacks Lamar and I carried, among other things, a frying pan, tin pieplates to eat off, lard, bacon, a bottle of iodine (which Aunt had insisted on), a small hatchet, a coffeepot and three tin cups, meal, sugar, coffee, three big cans of pork and beans, a bar of soap (Aunt again)—and unknown to anybody but ourselves a bottle of scuppernong wine and a pack of cigarettes. King carried nothing except himself, and as our loads grew heavier and bulkier, I envied him his dogdom. Little knowing how he irritated me, he'd run off into the fields on both sides of the road, carry on an investigation, and come back with a look on his face that said it wasn't possible to guess what wonders he'd seen and smelled. We shifted our sacks and plodded on.

When we got there, Uncle had discreetly gone home by another way than the one we had hiked. We found Hubby sweeping the shack clean, and the supplies Uncle had brought. Aside from what I've mentioned they included a pineneedle basket full of eggs, a chicken Aunt had roasted, six apples, a wedge of fruitcake, and about two dozen cold biscuits. Whatever happened, we would not starve. It was a fine day. We tramped the dry woods, laughing and making jokes, and being happily quiet at times. We climbed trees. We ran. We invented games and abandoned them for others before they had palled. We found a beehive, but didn't bother it. We chased King, and let King chase us. Lamar and Hubby fished and caught four, plus one early eel, who had himself unwisely felt the call of spring in the warming water. Just to breathe the clear, piny air was a blessing.

When night fell (earlier than we thought it would, for we were spring and it was winter), we built a fire in the fireplace. We fried the fish and eel and ate them with cold pork and beans and corn bread. We drank scalding-hot, sugared black coffee with our supper. King had biscuits mostly, and he grumbled a little, being used to better, until we gave him some of the roasted chicken.

After supper we went out and looked at the moon, but we came in soon, because there was getting to be something spooky about it out there. The moon made the bare winter field look pale, almost white. Except for the pines, the trees, which we'd seen only by daylight, their gray trunks softened and warmed by the sun, were stark and skeleton-like, with brittle branches reaching up toward the sky like the hands of beggars. The thick green needles of the pines had turned black by night, and the wind in them seemed to tell of death and eternal aloneness.

Without consulting, Lamar and Hubby and I banged the wooden shutters to, closing us in snugly. Hubby and I made up the pallets while Lamar built up the fire. King was tired. He flopped down in front of the fire, letting sparks fall on him without moving back.

Lamar got out the bottle of wine; I opened the cigarettes and passed them around. King snored, dreaming. His legs began to kick and he snuffled his muzzle in a dream-bark we could hardly hear. Hubby, who had seen him do this many times before our own fireplace at home, cocked his head, listening.

"I think he hears something."

Lamar said, "He's just chasing rabbits in his sleep." Then nudging King awake with his foot, "Aren't you, King?" King turned his head, looked at Lamar solemnly, and went back to sleep. Lamar poured wine into the tin cups and we lit cigarettes.

"Anybody heard any jokes lately?" Lamar asked.

"Yes," I said. "I have. Jesse James got on this train to rob it, and when he came to a certain old maid—"

"We heard it," Lamar and Hubby interrupted me together.

"Well, there's this one. A traveling salesman came to the farmer's house one night and asked if there was any place he could sleep. The farmer said sure, if you don't mind sleeping with my daughter. And the traveling salesman—"

"If that's the one about the silk handkerchief," Lamar said, "I told it to you."

It was, he had. But it wouldn't have hurt him to listen to it again. After all, we'd told it over and laughed at it a hundred times before. No, Lamar was cross, out of sorts.

Maybe scared? To tease him if he was, for cutting my joke off, I said, "I'll tell a ghost story."

Hubby put his wine down and ducked his cigarette, saving the duck for later. He stretched out on the pallet—we still had our clothes on—and reached a hand toward King who woke briefly and licked it. Maybe Hubby was scared, too.

"You don't know any ghost stories," Lamar said quite brusquely, "except the ones I told you."

"Yes, I do, I made this one up." I puffed my cigarette and sipped my wine, trying to look mysterious. "I made it up out of *true* things I've heard. There was once a beautiful, beautiful girl who lived in an old Southern mansion, outside of town on a high hill. Down below the cotton fields and the cornfields and the sweet-potato patch there was a steamy swamp with giant cypress trees all covered with long gray moss that reached right down to the water and dribbled in it."

Hubby raised his head from the floor. "Where was this?"

"Never mind. Let me tell it." Lamar's face brooded behind his cigarette smoke. "She lived in this great big house that had long, dark, creepy halls and cobwebs all over everything. The house was full of faithful, devoted colored slaves—"

"Slaves?" Hubby asked, frowning.

"It was before the War Between the States," I said.

"Well, how come if it's got all these devoted slaves they're cobwebs all over the place?"

"Are you going to let me tell it?" I asked tartly.

Hubby didn't say he would, but he subsided with a sigh,

changing his position, putting his head against King's flank, and looking into the fire.

"This rich, beautiful girl," I continued, "lived in the big house with her father and all the slaves around them. Her father wasn't a real Southern gentleman. He had farms, dozens of them, but he was in business, too. So he decided, in order to get richer, that his daughter should marry a fat, middle-aged trader from Charleston who had a lot of money he'd made out of selling slaves and tobacco." Hubby grunted doubtfully.

"The rich fat man from Charleston came to visit, but the beautiful girl wouldn't even leave her room or come downstairs and see him."

"It ain't scary yet," Lamar said.

"Will you just shut up?"

"What this girl's name?" Hubby wanted to know.

"Sally."

He laughed. "You making it up! You thinking about Miss Sally at the schoolhouse!"

"I *am* not!"

"Well, go on," Lamar said irritably.

"I didn't mean," I said, "that she never left her room. She just didn't come down to see her fat old suitor from Charlotte. But after supper—"

"Wait a minute." It was Lamar. "You said before he was from Charleston."

"That's right," I said. "Charleston. I just wanted to see if you were paying attention. Well, after supper, when her father and the suitor were getting drunk on port wine in the library—" I paused and sipped significantly from my cup. "The beautiful girl who loved and was loved by her mammy whose name was Aunt Jane—"

"Did she dip snuff?" Hubby asked.

"It doesn't matter."

"Mixture of yellow Buttercup and black Bruton with the red label?"

"Hush," I said. Hubby giggled into King's side, and King farted, still asleep, or pretending to be, because at home he had sometimes been shown to the door by Aunt when he broke wind.

I went ahead. "When they were drunk in the library, Aunt Jane would help her slip down the back stairs through the kitchen and out into the yard. Oh! It was beautiful at night. The moon shining on the magnolia trees and cape jasmine! There she'd meet her real sweetheart, a poor man from the town nearby, but very good-looking, and they were passionately in love."

Lamar stirred. "Was he an aviator?"

"This was before the War Between the States!"

"Oh, that's right," Lamar said, his interest slipping.

"One thing this sweetheart of hers liked to do was walk with her in the grounds among the sweet-smelling magnolias and cape jasmine, and he'd ask her to take the combs out of her long black tresses and let it all fall down below her waist—" When they looked startled, I said, "To her feet. It didn't drag the ground, but only just cleared it."

Hubby said, "That girl needed bobby pins."

"Hush awhile," Lamar said, getting more interested.

"One thing he liked to do," I continued, "was to take the combs out of her hair *himself*, and when it fell all around her, run the combs through it, combing it. Well, they went on like that as long as they could, although they knew their love was hopeless. They thought about running away, but they didn't have any money, and the beautiful girl couldn't run very fast because she was a little lame in one leg and got tired easy. Not lame enough for it to show except to somebody that knew, but lame enough to keep her from being very fast on her feet. Then her father said she had to name the wedding date to the suitor from Charleston. She wouldn't, so he did.—I forgot to say, there was a great big bell tower right in the middle and on top of the house, to call the slaves in from the fields at mealtimes and at sundown. That was a favorite place the beautiful girl liked to go and sit and read poetry when she was by herself and couldn't think of anything else to do. The day of the wedding came. Aunt Jane had made the wedding dress and baked a lot of cakes for the wedding, chocolate, devil's food, Japanese fruitcake. And several chocolate pies as well. All the buggies and wagons and fine carriages were coming through the gate and up the long drive. The bride-to-be had been dressed up and then left all alone, at her request, when suddenly—everybody heard the bell ringing in the tower!—Somebody ran up to it fast. And sure enough, there they found the beautiful girl who had hanged herself on the bell in the bell tower with her long beautiful black tresses."

I paused, finishing my scuppernong wine, to complete silence in the room. "And they say," I continued, "that every year on the anniversary of the girl's wedding day to the fat man from Charleston, the bell is heard ringing in the tower—and sometimes on moonlight nights people declare they've seen the ghost of the beautiful girl, pacing back and forth in the garden under the sweet magnolia, the combs out of her hair, her hair drooping down to her ankles, waiting for her true lover."

I finished, and with an artist's relish at my performance, which I knew had gripped them finally, I lit another cigarette, my second of the evening. King, who had not listened to my story but had lain sleeping throughout it, woke, shook himself, stood tensely, as if listening to sounds we were incapable of hearing, of another, a nether land. He sat on his haunches, looked into the fire, then lifted his head and howled. Wolves in the wilderness could not have made a more desolate, more mournful sound.

Hubby sat up and gripped himself. Lamar strode to the door and flung it open, listening. We were all, even the fire, suddenly quiet. Woods are not silent at night. Above many ordinary, known sounds rose a particular one.

"It's like a baby crying," Lamar said.

"A baby *dying*," I said.

"It's an owl," Hubby said. "A screech owl."

King trotted outside, paused in front of the door, and sat again on his haunches. Raising his head, again he howled.

"What you reckon he sees?" Hubby said.

"They don't have to see, they hear things we can't."

"I wonder what," Lamar said.

"Dogs know things," Hubby declared. "King does. He knows a lot of things people don't. Even I don't always know what he means. What if he's warning us?"

The wind had risen. We stood shivering a minute. None of us wore a sweater.

I said, "I wonder if anybody ever died in this room."

Lamar said, "I don't like it."

"King!" Hubby demanded. "You shut up and come back in here to the fire." Instead of King's coming in to us, we went out to him.

I looked back into the room. The wind raised the corner

of the nearest pallet. "The fire looks like it's dying," I said.

"King!" Hubby called. King had trotted a few yards away. He turned his head and looked at us as if he'd never seen us before. Then he faced back into the night, raised his head, and began a low grumbling in his throat, raising the pitch of it gradually to a howl that seemed to involve his whole body, down to the end of his toes and stub tail.

As if answering King, the cry in the woods sounded again. It could have been distant or near. It was probably an owl, as Hubby had suggested. A gust of wind banged the door behind us and scattered the last sparks of the wood coals up the chimney. The fire was dead. The moonlight, contrarily, no longer seemed bright. Each of us was wrapped in a cloak of fear. What frightened Hubby, I didn't know. Perhaps Lamar remembered the night in the cemetery when he had broken his father's tombstone. I remembered something I hadn't for a long time, two closed coffins, a smell of flowers that gripped heart and throat, the feeling of confusion more than grief, of being totally alone before Aunt and Uncle came.

"Let's go home!" It was I who voiced it, and though the others didn't answer, I knew their thoughts echoed mine.

"Wait a minute," Hubby said. He slipped into the house; we heard a faint sizzle and smelled wet ash smoke. Hubby returned. "Threw the coffee on the fire."

King whimpered urgently beside us. "Let's join hands," I said.

We did, I in the middle. From joining hands we locked elbows for greater closeness. But as we walked faster and lost step with each other, we relaxed our hold on one another and began to trot, then to run. There was enough moonlight for us to follow the rutted road out from the woods and across the rough field. Hubby and Lamar ran easily along the dry ruts on either side. I sometimes stumbled on the stubbled ridge in between. King ran ahead, not leaving us, as he easily could have, but leading the way. We reached the main road panting, but did not stop.

We pounded down the road, King ahead of us, white as a phantom dog, holding his speed to our pace.

Gasping, I felt that I would suffocate, that I could not run farther. But I could not, must not, stop. Trying to keep up, I dropped behind. I hadn't breath to call to them. The dark terrors we had known alone and never told each other had caught up with us suddenly. It was a matter of escape and survival, and each must be his own savior or be vanquished by his own ghost.

The road dipped down to a hollow where there was a short wooden bridge across an almost dry stream. I remembered it from our hike out that day. Trees hovered over the bridge, darkening it, and when I came to it, I stopped. In the shadows I listened to myself trying to get breath, but I was no longer afraid. I was as beyond fear as I was beyond hope. The things in the dark were welcome to come and get me. I didn't care. Hubby and Lamar had rounded the bend on the other side of the bridge and were out of sight. I was alone. In a few minutes my breathing returned to normal.

I started off to round the bend. Almost before I knew what it was running toward me, King had found me, jumping, scolding, ecstatically anxious to show he had not deserted me. I comforted him, and we walked on side by side until we were caught in the headlights of a car. It stopped. Leaving the motor running, Uncle jumped out and then stood still, looking at me and King.

"You all right, boy?"

"Yes, sir." King and I went up to him.

He didn't laugh. If he had, I think I'd have understood why, but I'd have turned and run back toward the house in the woods. King butted his head against Uncle in a friendly way. When Uncle spoke again, his voice was quiet and normal. "Want to go home?"

"Yes, sir."

We got into the front seat, King between us. "Where're Hubby and Lamar?" I asked.

"Waiting a little way ahead. I didn't stop, I just slowed down. We'll pick them up when we go back." He paused. "You mind going to the house out there just for a minute? I want to see to the fire."

"I don't mind. Hubby put the fire out before we left."

"We better check it."

He drove slowly along the road we'd run so fast. It was just a country road, like any other at night. When we came to the little house, he left the motor running, took a flashlight, and went inside. King and I stayed in the car, rocking lightly with its vibration.

He came back. "All out. That was smart of Hubby."

"Hubby's smart."

"Yes," he said.

He reached into his pocket and held out a pack of cigarettes. "Want one?" I hesitated. "I know it's something you'd rather do off by yourself or with the other boys, but come on." He laughed softly. "I'm not all that old either."

I fumbled in the pack for a cigarette. He took one, struck a match, and lit both. After a minute he said, "I wasn't coming out to pry in your affairs, understand. Your Aunt got anxious, so I offered to look in and see how you were."

After another minute I found it easy to say, "It was fun, Uncle, until the last part. That was my fault. I told a ghost story."

His tone was carefully without humor when he said, "It must have been a good one."

I laughed first. "Yes sir, I guess it was." He laughed and knuckled my head with a hard scrape.

Just as we got back to where Lamar and Hubby stood waiting, alert and nervous by the side of the road, Uncle said, "Ask Lamar to sleep over at our place. No need to get his mama and Johnny-May in a cackle tonight."

Chapter 13

In their long life together I don't think Aunt has had to fault Uncle for a single big thing, any more than he has had to fault her. But if one thing strained her at times, it was the undeniable fact that he had an eye for the girls. He must have been handsome then; he is now. I can see it now; I couldn't then—he was Uncle.

At gatherings, no matter how interestedly he started in to talk crops and politics to the men, he soon found himself with the women, dancing or joking or just talking. This was a little remarkable because in small-town society married people tended to segregate themselves by sex for conversation. When Aunt looked at a man, I think she saw no more than another fellow creature, pleasant or not to look upon, as he was amiable or not. When Uncle looked at a woman, he saw a woman, and the woman knew she had been seen. He wasn't a flirt, if I can say so at this distance, but his pleasure in the company of women was open and obvious. He never talked to me about this, of course, and I don't think he talked to anyone else about it either. For a man who was most generally liked, he had no intimate friends among men. I think the only intimate friend of his life has been Aunt, and I don't suppose his feeling about women was a thing they could have talked about. It must have been for him one of those vast, important areas of wonder and aloneness all of us have and cannot ask anyone to share.

Because Uncle acted contrary to local custom at parties, as he did indeed in other situations of life, he was sometimes misunderstood by those who did not know his ways. I don't mean that he caused jealousy among the husbands, but I've seen a husband look at his wife and Uncle in easy conversation with a look on his face that asked what in the world could any man find to say to her?

No, the misunderstandings came from an occasional unmarried girl who, flattered at Uncle's attention, assumed that he meant more than he did. That winter he and Aunt, both of whom loved any kind of dancing, took to going to square dances around the country. They had gone to a lot of them in their youth, but fallen out of the habit. Now they took it up again.

Uncle was an expert caller, but he preferred to dance. Sometimes he did both. He danced gaily, with great vigor; he loved to swing a partner up off the floor and laugh. Yes, I suppose in his dancing Uncle did flirt; it's a part of dancing if you take any real interest in it.

Aunt was as good a dancer as Uncle. I often saw him look at her with pride as she danced. Neat and precise in her ordinary daily movements, Aunt was surprisingly free, even abandoned, in her dancing. She did love it. Since they often took me with them—I learned to square dance at eight, although children were not often allowed in the adult sets—I used to watch them, sweating and smiling from their exertion and pleasure. I remember thinking that Uncle was still himself, but that Aunt wasn't *like* that. The ignorance of youth did not quite allow the woman who sometimes gave me calomel and castor oil to dance with Aunt's full-hearted enjoyment. I even wondered vaguely if God might not have something to say about that in His Bible.

They were gay parties, people arriving in wagons and cars, men and women in fresh clothes rustling with starch, the women powdered, sometimes with flour if they had no real face powder. The flour, of course, tended to make rings of dough on their necks when they began to sweat in the dance. After a set it was usual for the women to go off to the kitchen to repair their make-up, while the men drifted into the yard to refresh themselvs with a drink of whisky from bottle or jar, and perhaps to tell a joke they couldn't tell in front of their women. I stayed with the other children who had been brought along. Sometimes we watched our elders, or danced part of a set in a corner. Sometimes we went into another room to play. The dances were always held in someone's house, never in a barn, as the custom perhaps was elsewhere. The furniture would be cleared from the largest room and meal sprinkled on the wooden floor to provide a better sliding surface. Occasionally powdered wax was used, but people complained that it made the floor *too* slippery. They preferred meal, which at the end of an evening would be black from the dirt of shoes. If

I got sleepy before the dancing was done, I flopped on a bed and slept until Aunt and Uncle were ready to go. Sometimes five or six children lay stretched out on top of the same bed, dead to the noise of fiddle and shout and laughter from the next room, one oil lamp attending their sleep. Often Uncle picked me up, slung me over his shoulder, and carried me, still half-asleep, to the car for the drive home.

There always seemed to be more women than men at the parties. In my mind now I see a parade of those girls, fresh-looking and eager to have a good time. Every girl had a season in which she bloomed. Pretty or not, and they all seem pretty in memory, they carried at a certain time a special glow of life. Generally, by the end of that season, they were married.

There was one who was not; she carried her glow longer than the others and seemed in no hurry to marry, although she had beaus aplenty. Her first name was Bernice, and I don't remember her last. She was the daughter of one of the farmers Uncle knew, not on one of his farms. She was a pretty thing, full-bosomed and curved, and she wore her dance dresses tight, whether from necessity or design I did not know. She laughed a lot, but when she wasn't laughing, she looked at you—men, that is, even me—with a look that dared you to do all kinds of things. She danced like a gypsy.

I had got to know her a little the summer before, riding around the country with Uncle. He stopped at farms other than his own to talk weather and crops. Bernice always made over me a lot, telling me and anyone in earshot that I was one cute little boy, and she just might wait for me to grow up so she could marry me. Of course, that tickled me, and I often urged Uncle to stop at their place when it was not perhaps on his mind to do so. However, he seldom said no to me about that.

I suspect that Bernice worked hard on the farm and, in spite of the beaus, her only social pleasures were those dances and going to church. Her father's farm was not a prosperous one, and she was the only daughter. There was a sour-faced older brother, but he didn't like dancing and didn't come to parties often. If she couldn't get a ride with anyone else, he'd bring her and leave her for somebody else to take home. It was almost on our way, so Uncle fell into the habit of offering Bernice a ride. She'd pile into the back seat with me, tired and happy, but still not too tired.

If I were asleep or half-alseep, she'd pull me over against her for warmth and comfort. She smelled good, and I liked being close to her. A couple of times she kissed me, not quite the way a grown girl kisses a boy. Once, after she'd done so, I reached up and squeezed a titty. She laughed and shook my hand away, but she didn't tell. It was my first experience, although I didn't know it then, of back-seat cuddling. I felt very bold, although now I know that Bernice's cuddling me was simply a substitute for cuddling Uncle. For as time passed it was plain as day to everybody, including me—but not Uncle, it seemed—that Bernice was in love with him.

Every chance she got, and she didn't care who saw her, even Aunt, she stood close to him, laughing up to him, sometimes even bumping or rubbing against him in play. It would have taken a stronger man than Uncle to have altogether resisted Bernice. Certainly he did not. He laughed with her. He loved dancing with her; they made a handsome, spirited pair. And sometimes when they were just standing and she bumped him, telling a joke maybe, he bumped her back. I don't know what Bernice had in mind. Innocently: marriage? Or just a piece of fun?—I don't know. But I began to blush for her and for Uncle. And when I saw the sly looks of the others and saw from Aunt's burning frown that she saw, I blushed agonizingly for Aunt.

From liking Bernice I took a violent dislike to her. I decided she was tacky and two-faced and said so, which pleased Aunt, although she told me mildly that I wasn't to pass comment on grown people, it was sassy. I would no longer let Bernice pull me over to her on the back seat on the drives home. When she tried to, I pretended to be sleepy-cross and put my feet up on the seat between us, my head at the end of the seat by the open window. In addition to disliking her because of Aunt, I felt she had betrayed me. She had pretended to like me, but it was only because of Uncle.

One night Bernice overstepped. When we drove her home, she got out of the car, but instead of saying good night she exclaimed, "Oh, it's dark! It's pitch black! I don't know if I can find my way to the door!"

Uncle said gaily, "Maybe I'd better help you!" and got out of the car. It's possible he'd had a drop too much that night and not danced it all off, although he seemed sober enough, just a little high-spirited. I pretended to be asleep, although I was wide-awake and furious with Bernice. Aunt said not a word, but she watched, as I did. I was jealous of both of them, but I hated Bernice because she seemed to threaten Aunt—and me—and even Hubby and King, I remember thinking: What if Uncle decided he liked her better than us?

It wasn't as dark as Bernice had said. I could see them clearly as they went up the path, and of course Aunt could. Bernice stumbled, or pretended to, laughed, and hugged Uncle around the waist. They made one figure as they went up the path. At the steps she turned, flung her arms around Uncle, and gave him a big kiss right on the mouth. He came down the path slowly after she'd gone inside, and when he got into the car, he said nothing.

Aunt said, "Wait. Don't drive off yet." She got out of the car, slammed the door hard, and went up the path. It wasn't too dark for her to see; *she* didn't stumble. She went up the steps and knocked at the door. It opened presently and Bernice stood there with an oil lamp in her hand. I could see Aunt clearly. "Bernice, you seem to have taken too strong an interest in my husband. In future you must not count on us for a ride." Bernice had not a word to say, and if she did, Aunt didn't wait. She flicked her shawl and gathered it tighter about her shoulders, and came down the path, leaving Bernice at the door with the lamp showing her face. Aunt got into the car. "If I was wrong," she said, "go and tell her. She's still waiting." Uncle started the car and drove away fast. Pretending sleep more than ever, I hugged myself with pride in Aunt.

After a mile or so Uncle ventured to say, "I think you misunderstood. You surely can't suppose I—"

Aunt cut him off. "No such thing." There was a trace of crying as well as anger in her voice when after a minute she said, "Damn you. She's a poor, ignorant girl, but you should know better."

When we drove under the oak trees and stopped, at home, I let myself appear to wake up. "Good night!" I said and got out of the car and ran for the house, leaving them alone. A light was on in the living room. I went straight through the house to my room, turning on the light there and opening the door to the back porch. King was waiting, awake, having heard the car. I undressed quickly, and King and I hopped into bed. We were safe. I must have gone straight to sleep; I didn't hear Uncle and Aunt come in, although it was their habit to go all over the house after an evening out to see that everything was all right.

The next day was Sunday. Aunt was up early, singing in the kitchen, so I knew everything was all right. Uncle came in after I did. He gave Aunt an unaccustomed kiss on the cheek when she poured his coffee, and she blushed. When we all sat down to the table of steaming platters and bowls, he said with only a shade of a smile, "Maybe I'll go off to church with you." Beaming, Aunt pressed the tines of her fork into an egg, flooding her grits with delicious goodness. Uncle and I did the same. When I think of that scene now, I feel, in addition to some amusement: poor Bernice, poor Uncle.

Chapter 14

SPRING CAME, and it seemed to me I had never loved everything and everybody so much. In a few months I would be nine. Every day I felt older, and at that age to feel older every day is a step up instead of down. I looked back to a year ago and hardly acknowledged the child I had been as myself. Remembering Noochy brought a sharp but transient sadness. I was doing well in third grade. Miss Featherstone no longer seemed the ogre she had been last September. She even sometimes, when we had been good and lessons had gone well, spent the last part of the school day reading aloud a chapter of *Robinson Crusoe*, which all of us loved.

There was a time people thought country and small-town schools provided poor education. Perhaps. I don't agree. I had two or three teachers in that school who were as dedicated as any I was to find later in schools of larger reputation—unmarried women who cared about children in an unsentimental way, who cared about teaching, and knew how to make you remember things. It interests me to note that some of their methods are now being re-examined and put to use again. In any event, Miss Featherstone was such a dedicated teacher, the first of the several I was to know who carried me along with them, helping me to see and understand something about life and literature. Later, in college, I was to be puzzled at the difficulty a fellow student sometimes had over a matter that Miss Featherstone or Miss Sproull had made clear to me in the third or fourth grade. We learned from them, and we learned from each other. Windows and doors were left open; the air inside smelled as good as that out, and it had further the now exciting school odors of chalk and ink.

As the days began earlier, I got up earlier, often having two whole hours before school with King and Hubby, and sometimes Lamar, to rush about laughing like a fool, to note the appearance of each new bud and branch. Hubby and I were together more than Lamar was with either of us. Lamar was friendly, but he seemed to have less time for us just then. Always quick in schoolwork, he was studying harder than ever, especially science and mathematics. Lamar was going through that time when arithmetic mysteriously expands into mathematics, and he was beginning to be more aware of the difference in his and my ages. He talked seriously of becoming an aviator, and Uncle said he would help him any way he could.

Hubby had settled in with us completely. He no longer seemed nervous about the past, before he found us, nor apprehensive about the future. We would all go on as we were, I felt, only getting a little older—I was eager for that—but everything would stay much the same.

There was a huge log in our back yard that had been in the same position ever since I came there to live. It had no practical use. Uncle had brought it home from one of his cuttings of timber to show off its size. I liked to play on it, or sit on it and read. It made an excellent permanent board for watermelon cuttings. I still have a small photograph of me and King sitting on the log, taken about that time. The log was so big my legs reach down only halfway to the ground.

One morning when I woke early, King was sitting in front of the screen door that led onto the back porch. The door was latched, but the heavier door had been left open the night before because the weather was mild. King was looking out with more than his usual alertness. When he saw me awake, he began to growl. I told him to hush, and I dressed without bothering to discover what particularly interested and disturbed him outside. I thought perhaps a neighbor's dog had entered our yard on his morning round of inspection.

When I was ready to go and had my hand on the latch to lift it and let King out ahead of me, I looked into the yard for the first time. To my astonishment there on *my* log sat two men, gazing at the house, almost at me, I thought. They were dressed alike in overalls, denim shirts, old felt hats, and heavy shoes.

One of them was Toll Weaver. The other was a big colored man I'd never seen before in my life. I thought at first he might be one of the hands from the mill, but another look told me he was not. I knew them all. How dared

Toll come into our yard before we were up, and make himself at home! He knew what we thought of him, as we knew what he thought of us. And he didn't know that he mightn't find King loose, King who had hated him ever since that day in the barbershop. What could have made him so bold?

King gave me a scuffle, but I managed to push him back into the room and close the heavy door when I went out onto the porch. My bedroom was off the part of the porch that was screened, where the icebox stood and where we often ate in summer, so I had another screen door to pass before I was on the steps and they could see me.

"Morning, Mr. Weaver," I said, without courtesy. "What do you want?"

His face lit up in the happiest smile I had ever seen on it. "Want to see your uncle!" he called. The colored man said nothing. He looked at me, then looked around the yard.

"What do you want to see him about?" I asked.

"We'll wait," Toll said agreeably. "He's here, ain't he?"

"Yes."

"That's why we come early. To be sure and catch him before he got off on his rounds."

"You want me to get him up?" I asked.

"Whatever you feel like. We ain't in a hurry." Toll grinned at me and turned his head to speak to the other man. I could hear King in my room making a racket against the door. He must have recognized Toll before I shut him up.

The colored man said, "Where's Hubby?"

The reason for their appearance was instantly clear to me. I didn't know how they had come together, but I knew the big stranger was the thing Hubby feared and had run away from.

As I ran, banging doors, through the kitchen and into the main hall, I met Uncle. King must have wakened him. "What's going on?" He wore shoes and pants, and he was buttoning his shirt. He went quickly past me, and I followed him into the yard.

"Morning!" Toll said when he saw Uncle. He and the man kept their seats.

"Well?" Uncle said. "What is it?"

"We got a little business to talk over with you," Toll said.

"I don't do business with you, Toll."

"This time you may have to."

The colored man asked again, "Where's Hubby?"

Uncle said, "Both of you get off that log and stand on your feet like men, if you want to talk to me."

They looked at each other and slid to the ground.

Toll put on his smile again. "We don't want to start off unfriendly."

"Who is he?" Uncle said to Toll.

"I'm Hubby's daddy," the man answered for himself.

Uncle paused, thinking, then said to me, "Go get Hubby. We'll see."

As I ran off to the barn I heard Toll say, "Now that's brisk and businesslike. We're going to get along fine."

I don't know what was said while I was gone, and I wasn't away more than a minute. I didn't tell Hubby who was there, just told him Uncle wanted him. He was up and dressed and making his bed. When I got back to the yard, Uncle was asking the same question I'd wondered. "How did you two get together? Hubby's never said anything about family."

"I'll bet," the stranger said and grunted.

"A word of explanation is in order," Toll allowed. "I was over in Wadley yesterday on a little piece of business, and I heard there was this fellow been asking for his boy that run away from home. Boy's name was Hubby, they said, and I said I knew of such a Hubby. Being a father many times myself, I know something of the family tie, so out of kindness and wanting to help everybody to a happy ending I found the fellow and brought him over with me."

Hubby came out of the barn. When he saw who was there, he stopped; then he came on again until he was beside me and Uncle, facing Toll and the man who was obviously not a stranger to him.

Uncle said to Hubby, "This man says he's your daddy."

Hubby stared at the ground, refusing to look up.

"Is he?" Uncle said; his voice sounded gruff.

Hubby panicked and ran. He ran fast toward the wooden gate, but Toll who must have expected such a move was there before him, caught him and pushed him back toward where we were standing.

"Don't lay your hands on him!" Uncle ordered Toll. Then to Hubby he said, "Come here, boy. Don't go crazy. We'll figure it out. Just tell me."

Hubby looked up at Uncle. "He's my pa."

The man said, "My name's Vernon Lovelady. I got a farm up in Rupert County. Hubby ran away after his ma died. Just when he was getting big enough to be some help. So I been asking for him when I could spare the time, town by town, all the way down from Rupert County."

"Is he right, Hubby?" Uncle said. Hubby jerked his head once, affirmatively.

"It's a reunion of father and son," Toll said, grinning. "Don't it do your heart good?"

Vernon Lovelady said, "Come on, Hubby, let's get going."

"Wait," Uncle said.

"You can't go interfering in family matters!" Toll blustered. "Even if they are just colored. A daddy has his rights, and the boy ain't near grown."

I heard a noise like King's nails on the porch linoleum and turned. Aunt had let him out of my room, and they were standing together back of the screen door, King dancing lightly, wanting to come out.

"Why'd you run away?" Uncle asked Hubby. Hubby began to tremble, looked straight at his father for the first time, then looked away. Uncle put a hand on Hubby's shoulder to steady him.

"He beat me," Hubby said simply.

Toll laughed. "Bet it was nothing to what you'll feel when he gets you home! The idea a boy running off just when he gets big enough to be some help around a place. It's unnatural and sinful!"

Vernon said, "Come on, Hubby. Time to go."

Aunt couldn't resist crying out, "You can't let them!"

Without turning to her Uncle said, "Stay in there and keep King with you."

Aunt stooped to hold King, who had begun to growl menacingly when she spoke.

"I can't let you have him," Uncle said to Vernon.

Vernon scowled, looking perplexed for a moment. "He's mine. He belongs to me. I'm taking him back, peaceably if he'll come peaceably, with a stick if he won't."

"That's only right!" Toll said to Uncle. "You know you *daren't* stop a man collecting his own boy that run away from his own home! Not even you with all your big airs."

"Come on, Hubby," Vernon said.

Hubby spoke to him directly for the first time. "I'll run away again, first chance."

"Maybe I won't give you a chance," Vernon said. "Maybe I'll lock you up when you ain't working."

"Oh, now that wouldn't be *nice!*" Toll said with elation, drawing out the "nice" into several syllables. "I think everybody's getting a little bit excited—too excited if you want my honest opinion. There must be a solution, if only I can think of it." Toll pretended to think, pleased with himself, trying to build suspense. When he'd thought, he snapped his fingers over his conclusion. "Tell you what!" He turned to Vernon. "As well as being your own flesh and blood, he's valuable to you as a worker, ain't he?"

Vernon said, "He could do a day's work when he was a mind to."

"I did it all!" Hubby burst out. "I did everything, and you wouldn't give me a nickel to spend!"

"Whoever heard of paying your own chillun!" Toll said. "Just for doing their bound duty toward their daddy." His voice went confidential with Vernon. "I can see you got a case on your hands. He won't be easy to handle! Regular wild one. Probably wind up in the electric chair in Milledgeville."

Behind us I heard Aunt gasp.

"Heard you went off to look at it!" Toll addressed the porch. "Awful sight, they say!"

"Keep your talk to me," Uncle said curtly.

Toll smiled and addressed Hubby. "Come over here, boy."

Hubby didn't move.

"Come here," Vernon said. "I ain't going to put my fist to you."

When Uncle didn't stop him, Hubby moved over slowly to the two men, but stopped when he was still out of their reach. Toll smiled at him, as if with approval. "Get up on that log, boy!" Hubby looked puzzled but obeyed. When he had hopped up on the log he stood awkwardly with his arms dangling.

Toll gazed at him. "Fine working specimen of a boy! Little skinny, but can do a real day's work, his daddy says, and he ought to know! Look at him! A mite sullen and troublesome, but muscle on his arms and back, and that's where you look to find the worth!" He turned to Vernon, as if he had a sudden inspiration. "Why don't you sell him to these folks?"

Hubby ducked his head and tears started from his eyes just as Uncle shouted, "Get down from there, Hubby!"

Crying, Hubby slid down the log and came running at Uncle. Uncle caught him and held him against him. "Get off my place," Uncle said. "Both of you. I swear to God I'll kill you if you touch Hubby. I'll kill you with that ax, like I would a hog, and take the consequences."

Neither of them had expected that. Vernon began to

move slowly away, but Toll stopped him, speaking encouragingly and reasonably for all. "Maybe we went a little too fast. Not too far, mind you, but too fast for the delicate." He raised his voice to Uncle. "Don't you talk about killing! You got no rights in this case!" He relaxed himself, the picture of a crooked lawyer who, having no emotions himself when he is before a jury, can nevertheless assume them to suit his purpose. After a deliberate pause he looked at Uncle and smiled. When he spoke, his voice was that of sweet reason, oil on stormy waters. He cocked an eyebrow. "You want to keep the boy, you say, won't give him up. Right?" Uncle made no answer. Toll turned to Vernon. "And you *quite* rightly say he's your boy, which nobody denies, and that you want him to go home with you and help you farm your little place. All perfectly reasonable and understandable. You agree? Well, then, if you agree to let Hubby stay here, which would be mighty generous of you all around, these folks ought to be happy to pay you something every month—for the work he's doing for them and not for you." Toll studied the air. "What do you think is fair? As the honest dealer in this trade, I ought to get a little for my trouble. Let's say these folks pay you a hundred dollars a month to keep Hubby. I take twenty for my trouble and for keeping a watch here, and you get eighty."

Vernon tried to frown as if he were considering the proposition, but he smiled instead. Eighty dollars a month would make him rich. He wouldn't have to worry about his land.

Toll turned to Uncle. "How's that for fair?"

"I won't bargain," Uncle said. He turned his head toward Aunt on the porch. "Go to my desk and bring me a hundred dollars."

Aunt shut King back into my room and went for the money. No one spoke until she came back and handed it to Uncle.

Uncle started to give it to Vernon, but Toll's hand slid in and took it. He counted off twenty dollars for himself, carefully licking his fingers after touching every bill, and then he slowly counted out eighty dollars to Vernon.

"You see?" he said to Vernon. "I told you it'd be all right. These are nice folks to deal with." Vernon nodded. Toll turned to Uncle. "Now if you'll just do the same every month, I'll pass it along to Vernon, minus my little share, and everybody will be happy. If you don't, we'll have the law on you."

Hubby ran, boiling with shame, fast as he could tear, to the barn.

"Get!" Uncle said. "Both of you."

They went out the gate slowly to show they were not afraid. Toll latched it carefully, affecting a little trouble with the latch to take more time. "Have to keep that dangerous dog of yours locked up good, so he won't threaten any more people. Somebody might shoot him if he does. I'll be around to collect every month." Turning to leave, he laughed to himself. "I expect that little nigger'll go around bragging he's worth a hundred dollars! Will wonders never cease?"

They were gone. I went off to the barn to find Hubby. Aunt let King out and came from the porch to Uncle.

Hubby was quiet and kept mostly to himself that day. I

went off to school, and he and King met me as usual that afternoon to walk me and Lamar and Johnny-May home. I'd already told Lamar and Johnny-May what had happened, so none of us had much to say.

As we were about to part in the road between our houses, Johnny-May took one of Hubby's hands and yanked it hard before letting go. "Hubby, don't you run away fom us, you hear?"

Hubby laughed. "You're one crazy little girl! Now why would I do that?"

"I don't know," Johnny-May said. "Just don't."

"You mean you'd miss me?" Hubby teased her.

"Yes. I would." Johnny-May frowned earnestly.

Hubby laughed as if it were a joke, and we went into our yard with King and closed the gate.

After supper I usually went off to my room with King to study or read a book, and Uncle went to the living room to read his Atlanta paper while Aunt finished her work in the kitchen. But that night wasn't usual. Uncle got his paper from the living room and brought it into the kitchen to read while Aunt and Hubby did the dishes. I fed King on the porch and let him out to prowl. Then I got a book from my room and came back to the kitchen, too. When Hubby was hanging the dish towels to dry, Aunt took off her apron and said, affecting to be casual, "I think maybe Hubby ought to sleep in the house tonight."

"That's a good idea," Uncle said so quickly I knew he hadn't been reading his paper.

"Why don't you, Hubby?" I joined in.

Hubby laughed, but shook his head. "Don't any of you go worrying about Hubby. I'm all right down there. Won't anybody come to get me—they been, and they got what they came for. Good night!"

He left us quickly, letting the porch door slam softly behind him.

After a pause Uncle said, "I had a talk with him this afternoon. He wanted to just leave, but I think I talked him out of it. It hit him hard, their making him stand on the log like a slave at auction. It was mean, wicked. Hubby's proud. I finally got him to promise he wouldn't do anything sudden or rash."

Aunt was at the window looking toward the barn where a light showed. "I'll worry about him, but at least he promised."

Next morning King and I were up early and went to find him in his room in the barn. We found only Tom, sitting on the bureau looking displeased. Hubby was not there. His bed was made. There was a note on the table beside it. There was no salutation.

> *I have to break my promise. I have to go now, or maybe I couldn't. I can't let you pay for me, and I won't go back to him. I been happy with you all. I love you all. And King. Lamar and Johnny-May too. Say my name to King some time so he won't forget me too soon. Don't worry and don't try to follow because I don't know which way I go. Maybe west to be a cowboy. I talk to the hoboes when the freight train stop and they tell me a lot so I'll get along okay.*
>
> *Love from your friend Hubby*

Aunt cried off and on through breakfast, and I didn't have my mind on school that day. After school I walked home with Lamar and Johnny-May, but I left them in the road. King ran to meet me when I came through the back gate, happy to see me, puzzled at Hubby's absence, and apologetic about not meeting me after school. Aunt was sewing on the back porch, very busy and intent, as if her life depended on it. Mildred sat placidly beside her, frowning mildly into eternity. Uncle, I knew, was at the sawmill.

I went to the kitchen, pulled a cold biscuit apart and put a slice of cold fried ham between the halves. After biting into it I went on out and got King and we walked off through the back way and got to the railroad tracks, a little way out of town.

Maybe Hubby had hopped a freight train last night. Did he go this way or that? One way was almost west, so maybe it was the one he'd chosen. I tried to think of Hubby way out there already, riding the range on a faithful cow pony. After a while the thought was comforting. I bent my head to King's ear and said in an ordinary tone, "Hubby." He didn't wiggle or twist; he sat down on a tie between the rails. I sat down on a rail. We looked both ways. There was nothing coming and nothing going, but Hubby was gone.

Chapter 15

In spite of all the things we did that kept us busy, we missed Hubby. Uncle managed to accept his going, although it was a reluctant and angry acceptance, but Aunt kept hoping that Hubby would think better of what he'd done and come back. She and Johnny-May kept his bed made up fresh for a long time. Aunt washed and ironed his clothes and laid them in a drawer of the bureau in his room. (The room is used for storage now, but it's still referred to as Hubby's room.)

Every evening, just as it got dark, King would sit on the ground below our steps; he'd sit thinking hard about Hubby for a while, and then he'd lift his head and howl, as if he could reach Hubby that way and get him to come back. Nobody said anything about it the first three times it happened, but the fourth evening Aunt couldn't stand it any more. When King began to howl, she flew out of the kitchen and out the door. I followed her. When she got to

King she cried, "Stop it!" and kicked him. King turned a hurt and surprised face to her. She dropped to her knees and hugged him, saying in a steadier voice, "Don't do it. Don't do it again. It hurts me too much."

One of the cruelest things that ever happened was Aunt's losing her own child and not having another. She was a woman ripe with life, in spite of her particular ways. She had love and caring to spare for anything that needed her. That's why it was so easy for her to take to me, to Johnny-May, and to Hubby. To lose any of us would have been like again going through the loss of the child in the cemetery. God may know what He's about, but there are times I beg leave to differ.

Word got around town. Lamar and Johnny-May were talkers, and of course I had to tell my version, having been there when everything happened. None of us spoke to Toll, so none of us told him, but he heard, all right. One day when I was in the post office getting our mail, he was talking to his usual bunch of men loud enough to be sure I heard. He said he for one didn't believe that nigger had run off. Hell, why would he when he had white folks to give him any and everything he wanted? What's more, they were willing to pay his pa so they could keep him! Could you match that? The nigger was obviously hiding, or, more likely, being hid. They'd all see. He was himself going to work on the mystery. In the meantime he managed to stay drunk on the money he had made on the transaction.

The following Saturday morning Uncle asked me at breakfast if I'd like to go to the sawmill with him. I thought maybe he wanted me, so King and I went. There was no work at the mill on Saturday or Sunday, maybe a little tidying up on Saturday morning, but nothing serious. Uncle often slept late on Saturdays and went out mid-morning to pay the week's wages to the men. After that they were free until Monday and went into town or off to see their families. Most of them slept at the mill unless their families lived close. Transportation was not easy, and the hours of work were long then for everybody.

When we got out there, Uncle sat down in front of the cookhouse with his roll of work hours and wages earned opposite the names. He opened his wooden cash box and started paying off. I went into the cookhouse and passed some time with Cook. He was free most of Saturday and all of Sunday, too, of course, but he often stayed at the mill by himself. He didn't have much use for town. His being crippled made him shy with people he didn't know. So he acted as a kind of watchman for fires.

The men came up and claimed their pay, and there were jokes and pleasantries about what they'd be doing until Monday. They wandered off, and King and I wandered off, too. I stood for a minute looking at the wide, thick fan belts and at the sharp-toothed circular saw that cut the logs into planks with an angry-sounding high screech. When it was being operated, I stood well back, but when it was not, it fascinated me to stand close. I knew that a touch of the lever would set the saw into whirring life, ready for the trolley to send a log into its teeth. Then I went off looking for King.

I found him in the woods, and he and I roved around for a while. But it was quiet and a little spooky without the men cutting and sawing and calling to one another, so shortly King and I went over to the mountain of sawdust and began to play. The game was to try to run up it fast before your feet got bogged in sawdust, then to tumble down to the bottom, rolling over and over. It was hard for me to make the top, but I could do it with effort if I went fast enough. I had only two feet to King's four, bigger ones than his. King couldn't manage it at all, and he couldn't understand how I could do it and he couldn't. Of course, the more effort he expended with his small feet, the quicker and deeper he bogged. I'd stand at the top laughing at him and then start to roll and tumble down, catching him on the way. We'd roll all the way to the bottom of the hill, I laughing, King frisking and eager to try to climb it again. But I knew he never would, so after a game or two we'd go off to something else.

We did that Saturday. There were only two or three men left talking around the cookhouse when we went to the lumber piles to play. The game there was a very simple one of hide-and-seek, and King had long before mastered it. The planks were stacked in triangles. King would squeeze through an opening at one end and wait for me in the middle of the triangle. I had to climb one side of the planks and down into the well on the other, always to find King there barking, as if he had surely surprised me that time. Then after playing snap and tag a minute I'd climb up again and over to the outside. King was always waiting for me and barking in a pleased way, as if he'd been very clever to anticipate my plan.

We exhausted the simple mysteries of one pile of lumber and went on to another, as if it would be different, although both of us knew it would be just about the same as the one we'd left. We started the game again, but when

I dropped down inside, King was not there. I whistled for him before I saw the sleeping man. My whistle woke the man.

It was Toll Weaver. King must have seen him and gone to get Uncle. In all his life I had never seen King try to attack a person. The only report I'd had of such a thing was Hubby's of the events in the barbershop. People were for people to deal with. King bared his teeth only to other animals and only to them when they presumed to attack him, or when he was hunting with Uncle or Lamar.

Toll had been sleeping flat on the ground. The stiff weeds he'd been lying on sprang halfway erect when he lifted himself to a sit and focused his eyes on me. I'd had little experience of drunken men, but I realized Toll was, or must have been before sleeping, drunk. He said, "Well." And when he'd gathered his thoughts some more he said, "I come looking for Hubby." He got to his feet and stretched the cramps out of his big body.

Uncle appeared then, King trotting at his side. He looked at Toll with surprise, which seemed to turn Toll blue-mad. "I was asking your snot-nose boy where Hubby is. I know you got him hid somewhere, trying to do me and his daddy out of our little piece of money. I aim to find him and make you pay and keep on paying as long as he's yours!" I slipped around back of Uncle and King, who had begun to growl against his teaching.

"Come out of there," Uncle said.

"I ain't moving till I see Hubby."

"Hubby ran away."

"Don't tell *me!* A little nigger that's found a soft place ain't going to leave it. No, sir. Don't tell *me!*"

"I'm telling you to come out of there and go home."

"You and your big-ass airs! Sending your wife in the house for a hundred dollars as easy as I'd spit tobacco!" That had rankled, even though the money was for him. What he hated was Uncle's having it at all, but the way Uncle had requested it and handed it over were the final bricks in his house of hate. He spat close to Uncle's foot. "You've met your match today, and more than."

I think it was the spitting that made Uncle forget his reason. That immemorial childish gesture of insult can rouse the mildest man, and Uncle was not that. "For the last time, Toll, are you going to go, or am I going to have to make you?"

Toll visibly savored the moment of waiting before he said, "I'd say you're going to have to make me."

Toll came for Uncle fast, but Uncle was ready for him and landed his fist right in the middle of Toll's belly. Toll fell back a step or two to get his breath, then came on again.

"Keep out of it," Uncle said to me. "Get away."

Toll looked twice as big as Uncle in that small space. The next time he swung, Uncle couldn't dodge; he caught Toll's fist on the side of his head, and his ear started bleeding. He must have been dazed for a few seconds. He tried to grab Toll around his middle and trip him. They both fell, but Toll got free quickly and kicked at Uncle. Uncle rolled out of his way and got to his hands and knees. It was then I got truly scared. I saw that Toll might whip Uncle, and I couldn't stand by for that.

Leaving King, I ran to the cookhouse. I found Cook, but everyone else had gone. When I told him what was happening, he grabbed a butcher knife off his table and followed me in a limping run. Just before we got to the triangle where they were fighting, one side of the triangle flew loose. The two men and King fell out of it in a tangle. They broke apart and rolled away from each other to get to their feet again, but King grabbed Toll by one leg and bit him before Toll was able to kick him away with his other foot.

Panting, Uncle was yet able to say, "Somebody hold that dog off!" I knew why he bothered. If a dog attacked a man, he was generally killed.

Cook dropped his knife and grabbed King. King was still snapping and making a dangerous noise, but he knew better than to fight Cook. Cook threw him toward me and picked up his knife from the ground. It was all I could do to hold King, but I did. I don't think I could have if he hadn't been so used to minding me. I hit him across the muzzle to shock and calm him, as I'd seen Aunt do, but I kept talking to him.

Both men were on their feet but stayed for the moment well away from each other. Toll managed a short laugh, full of contempt and self-vindication when he saw Cook with the knife. "Trained your niggers to do your fighting?"

Uncle ran at him and hit him right where jaw joins neck. Toll spat red. He looked at the red spit a second and then jumped up and landed full on Uncle, knocking them both to the ground. For a minute they rolled and panted and cursed, making wordless noises of rage that were like King's when he was fighting. They were both dirty and bleeding. It was, in a way, like a rooster fight. The two would tangle, giving each other as much damage as they could. Then they'd separate, circle each other, and feint, panting, before they joined again. There was no mistaking that in their hearts it was a fight to the death.

Slowly they worked their way to the space between the cookhouse and the machinery, Cook and I edging along with them. Cook held his butcher knife so tight his knuckles bulged. He was ready to use the knife if the fight went the wrong way. King was still struggling with me and making a racket. It must have bothered Uncle, for he managed to say, "Shut King up!" He was gasping, almost sobbing, with fatigue. Whatever my hopes, and my prayers that were more like oaths, I knew that Uncle was losing the fight.

I tussled King over to the cookhouse and shut him inside. He was barking furiously. I was desperate, and I knew Uncle was. I didn't see how it could end, except in defeat for him, for us all. So I grabbed Cook by the hand not holding the knife and begged, "Go get help."

He looked at me a moment, staring like a man startled out of sleep. Then he understood that if Uncle were whipped, we were only a boy and a small crippled man with a knife. He dropped the knife and ran limping toward the car, I following.

"Get in, I'll crank," I said. I found the strength to in that moment, although I had never managed it before, and Uncle had always let me try. Presently the engine caught, and Cook turned the car in a big wide circle and drove away fast.

I was aware that King was still inside the cookhouse, still barking and throwing himself against the door, but my eyes and my mind were on Uncle and Toll. Sure of his advantage now, Toll toyed with Uncle. He let him get close and land an exhausted blow. Then he hit Uncle full in the face, not with all his strength because he wanted to draw the game out, but hard enough to send him to his knees like a drunken man praying.

Eventually Toll tired of his sport, or perhaps he simply tired. The next, the last time Uncle went for him, all he had to do was raise his leg and push Uncle with his foot. Uncle stumbled backward, fell, and did not get up. Toll went over to him and circled him. So did I, keeping out of Toll's way, not daring to help Uncle up. In a minute Uncle began to moan and stir. Toll lifted his foot—I couldn't believe it, I don't know why, considering what I had seen and knew about Toll—and very deliberately, taking his time, kicked Uncle hard in the head. Uncle rolled over on his face and began to vomit.

I was almost vomiting, too, as I grabbed Toll, kicking. I found an arm and bit into it, as if I were King. He shook me loose, as he had King, and gave me a slap that laid me on the ground. Uncle was unconscious. I sat up to see Toll dragging him over to the saw machinery.

When he found me looking at him, he stopped. "We're going to have a little accident." His mouth was still bleeding; there were cuts and dirt all over his face, but it was a face triumphant nonetheless. I knew then surely he was insane, for I knew what he planned to do. He lifted Uncle from the ground onto the trolley that took the logs down to the saw when the machinery was set in motion. It could be, I knew, set in motion by the simple throwing of one lever. Toll was going to kill us both.

King was still barking. I got up and ran toward the cookhouse to let him out, but Toll beat me there. Toll was good at knowing what you were going to do just before you did it. He slapped me again. "I can see I got to slap some more sense into you," he said. "After we do the Big Man, we'll see about you."

I got to my hands and knees, crying and crawling. Where was God, if Aunt believed in Him? I had seen Cook's butcher knife on the ground where he had thrown it as he ran to the car. It was a long knife, the top of its blade black with age, but the cutting edge of it underneath was clean and sharp.

Toll saw what I was up to, but too late to stop me. That was one time he hadn't guessed quick enough. By the time he got to me I was on my feet, the long knife in my right hand, the way I'd seen Cook hold it. He wasn't afraid of me, but he was nervous about the knife, and he stood off.

Seeing him do so I felt safer. "Take a step back."

He did. It was absurdly, horribly like a child's game Hubby and I had played with Johnny-May.

"Take another!"

He did, but he began to smile. "Who taught you to fight nigger fashion? That Hubby?"

"I don't care," I said. "If you come toward me a single step, I'll cut you!" I knew I had stopped him for a moment, but I was scared. I could only pray for time. As my own brief confidence faded, his confidence grew. He smiled.

"Time somebody taught you manners. You ain't going to cut me." His voice was so assured I knew that what he said was true. He took a step toward me.

"Get back!" I was the one to take a step back.

He took another step.

"I mean it!"

He laughed. "Sissy sassy little city boy!"

When he took a third step, I turned and ran—I didn't know where to—still holding hard to the butcher knife. I ran on, not looking back. He threw himself at me, tackling me. The knife fell. I was under him for a moment, but his fall had stunned him more than it had me, so I was able to squirm out from under him and run again. He followed as I ran for a stack of lumber, thinking if only I could get there and hide until somebody came. As he followed me closer and closer, I saw myself trapped, and I repeated the game I played with King. I quickly climbed one side of the triangle of planks and was out of his reach before he could grab my leg. But when I got to the top and was about to climb down on the inside of the triangle, he, like King, was waiting for me. I toed my way carefully along the swaying top board to another side, and he was there, easily. I did it again, and he was still there. He looked up at me grinning, the drying blood on his face making him look more fearsome than ever. He didn't dare come up, for fear of toppling the planks on himself, but neither could I come down without his getting me.

"Smart, ain't you?" He lifted his foot and pushed hard against the plank side I was on. It shook but did not cave in. Then angrily he threw his weight behind the shoulder he aimed at the piling of planks. As it crumpled, I jumped. I fell on my feet and rolled over. But not waiting for my shock and numbness to pass, I started running back toward Uncle and King.

Toll decided to give me up for the moment and to finish

Uncle. Uncle still lay on the log trolley as Toll had left him. Toll was making toward the switch. I opened the cookhouse door and King came out running. Whatever he saw or knew, he seemed to see only Toll. He ran for him.

For a man afraid of no other man, Toll was afraid of King. He threw the switch and turned to kick King off. But King would not be kicked off; he leaped high for Toll's throat. The heart-stopping screech of the saw was in my ears. King had not found his mark. Toll kicked him, and King leaped at him again. Kicking and unthinking, trying to get away from the dog, Toll hopped up onto the trolley, shoving Uncle off into the face of the dog. I ran to Uncle and King.

The saw was still screeching, and I was still holding onto Uncle on the ground trying to wake him up when Cook came back with two of the mill hands he had overtaken on their way to town. Somebody threw the switch and stopped the saw. In the sudden silence I looked up, and ever after wished I hadn't. Not even the war had a more grisly sight to show me.

The sheriff came over from the next big town—we weren't big enough to have one of our own—but whereas there was much to tell, there wasn't much to investigate. Even Toll's friends had nothing to say in his favor. His power was in his being alive. Now both pieces of him lay in the cemetery. We did not go to the funeral.

Toll's widow was not a bright woman, but she was smart enough to know she had been his slave and his victim. Miss Sally and Miss Featherstone took a strong stand in the matter. They got all of Toll's children back into school, except the oldest boy, who took over Lamar's job at the filling station after Uncle convinced Lamar that he needed him as co-foreman for his farms and the sawmill. Johnny-May became best friends with one of Toll's daughters next year at school. They played dolls together at the foot of Aunt's sewing machine, as Aunt made the foot pedal hum, making clothes for the Weaver children.

Chapter 16

THE CRASH and the Depression came later that year, and the town I lived in died. It's still there, but not as I knew it as a boy. They say that certain country towns in America set a pattern of life for themselves about 1870 and kept it until the Depression of 1929. Mine was one of them.

They were hard times. There was loss; there was sharing. Nothing was easy. I was too young to understand what was happening, but one event brought it home to me. Late in the fall Aunt had an all-day quilting party, such as was common enough in those days. A woman saved pretty scraps of cloth for a year or two, sewed them together into a pattern of her own making, and then invited women friends to spend the day and make a quilt. There was a good dinner, hard, steady work, and plentiful talk. I was old enough to feel a boy's horror at such women's gatherings, but I did not. The talk of women always fascinated me. Whereas men could spend hours being boring about the

Democrats and the Republicans, women talked about things that mattered: themselves and other people. So I went about my own business, but I was in and out of the house a lot after I came home from school. By then the quilting frame that had started out very large in the morning had contracted around the last center work of the quilt. Most of the guests were chatting at the side of the room, picking up bits of thread from the rug, discussing old gossip and speculating on new. Only four women were left at the frame, one of them a particular friend of Aunt's, Mrs. Fred Griffin Anthony (Aunt Phyllis to me). Coming into the room with the last pot of coffee and plate of cake for the day, Aunt said, "Phyllis, I've never seen you work so hard or be so quiet as you've been today. You're the one that usually ducks out of the hard work and keeps us laughing."

It was meant as a joke, but it was not that to Aunt Phyllis. From the doorway I watched her plunge her needle into the quilt and leave it there. She took off her thimble and her glasses, and dropping them into her lap, put her hands to her face and began to cry. Alarmed, Aunt went over to comfort her.

"I'm sorry," Aunt Phyllis said after a brief cry, dabbing at her eyes with a handkerchief she took from her dress pocket. "I shouldn't have come, but I wanted to. Fred told me last night the bank in Augusta where we keep everything failed. They closed up. They won't pay off."

Astonished, appalled, I saw handkerchiefs come out of the pockets of other women, until it seemed that half the guests assembled were crying and telling of similar disasters.

Miss Sally was one of those who cried. Her husband, Tom Paul, and Uncle were probably the most prosperous men about. They lost all they had except themselves and the land they stood on. The land couldn't be sold; there was nobody with money to buy it. The crops grown on it couldn't be sold either except at prices that meant a further loss. We were all poor.

We still went to the churches and sang and listened to the sermons. We celebrated Christmas and Easter, but in a shabbier way than before. We welcomed the newborn and buried the dead. We gossiped and worked. We had our parties still, poor as they were. But we were different. We did not perhaps grow harder, but we were watchful and anxious.

The only one of us who was not aware of hard times was King. Before, hunting and fishing had been sport. Now they were a necessary way to supplement our food supply. King had always been a good hunter. Now Uncle and Lamar took him out for an hour or two every day. If there was more fish or game than we could use, we passed it along to those who were glad to have it. They paid us back with other kindnesses. This sort of favor was remembered and repaid, not instantly, but in time, whereas before it was taken amiably for granted and often forgotten.

But it is not my purpose to tell about the Depression. Those who lived through it don't need telling; those who didn't don't care. My purpose has been to tell only about the town I knew as a boy, before it changed and became any town.

I am sure other boys have had dogs as good as King (I

don't really believe this), whom they loved as much as I loved King. I have given his name to these chapters, not because he was a hero, although he certainly saved Johnny-May from the snake and Uncle and me from Toll Weaver, but because when I remember old times, he always seems to have been part of them. Others may at moments have been more prominent actors; he seems the most constant and present—probably because he was the one thing in my early life that was more mine than anybody else's. We owned each other because we loved each other, with no questions, no doubts. To say that I was an insecure child or that he was only a dog begs the whole question of love. All love is based on need, and on a readiness to give and take.

It would not be difficult to fictionalize, to invent a last dramatic triumph and glorious death for King in the popular story fashion, but the truth is more satisfying to me. King lived happily ever after, or as near as anyone can. When I went away to school and then to the war, he still had Uncle and Aunt, and Tom's and Mildred's descendants who were much like them and fulfilled their old functions. He had the woods and the fields, the sawmill and the creek.

As he grew older Uncle still took him everywhere. King would ride on the front seat of the car beside Uncle, as his mother Queenie had, looking only a little milder, kinder, and more regal in his old age than he had when young. He welcomed my visits and missed me when they were over, Aunt said (her way of saying, too, that she missed me). But his was a good life. After I left home Aunt let him sleep in my room. She covered my bed with a special old quilt and even—she who would not pamper animals!—

gave him a pillow with a special case she had stitched with his name threaded on it.

Not wanting to sadden me, neither Aunt nor Uncle wrote to me during the war about how feeble King was getting. When at the end of it I went home to visit, King was there, as I had expected him to be. He could not run to meet me—he was eighteen years old—but he waited on the porch until I came to him from the car, looking happy and giving a slow twist of his old behind in greeting.

That afternoon, changed into civilian clothes, I borrowed Uncle's car and took a long, meandering drive, King on the front seat beside me. I said hello to people here and there, but I stopped with no one for long, except Mrs. Belser. She still had her novelty shop, although the icehouse had long been closed. Mr. Belser was dead, and she was on her own. When King and I left her, she gave him his usual pat and affectionate word, and she gave me a chocolate bar just as she and Mr. Belser had done all those years ago.

I paid no attention to the Salter place. Other people lived there now. Lamar had died during the war. Johnny-May had grown up and married her doctor. Mrs. Salter—Aunt May—died of cancer in 1943.

We went the long way past the cotton gin to the Milly Hole. I helped King out of the car and we walked down to it, but there was nothing to remind us of the happy days we had spent there. It was no longer used for swimming; the town had a swimming pool. The cable was gone, of course, and the log that used to be such a good thing to sit on and think about life had been washed away in a flood.

I found the little church and the churchyard Tussy was buried in, but I couldn't find her grave. After that, on the way home, I turned off the main road and drove through a field road and some woods to the house Lamar and Hubby and I had tried to camp in. The house was burned down; only the chimney stood. I had already talked to Aunt and Uncle about Hubby. No, he had never written, never come back to visit. Whatever his reasons, we were sure they were, for him, good ones.

We drove home late in the afternoon. King was tired and ate only a little of his supper. When I'd had a talk with Aunt and Uncle after supper, I found that I was tired, too. I said good night and went to my room. The bed was turned down. King was asleep on the floor beside it. He woke when I came in, yawned, and watched contentedly as I undressed.

"Tomorrow we'll be up early and we'll go everywhere," I whispered, just as I had done when we were both young. I lifted him to the bed, and he smiled at me, apologizing for his old age. When I turned out the light and got into bed, he turned around a couple of times in his old way before settling himself on top of the covers. I whispered into his ear, "Hubby?" He turned his head to me and licked my knuckles.

When I woke the next morning, he was dead.

Aunt cried and then said, "Well, he was waiting for you. He had to see you first. Poor dear soul; I'm glad he was able to wait. I'm cooking sausage as well as ham to go with your eggs. Is that all right?" She turned quickly to the stove.

I said that it sounded good to me and to call me when she and Uncle were ready. I went off to the barn to find a box that would do for my King. Nobody, I'm convinced, really accepts the death of something he loves. But I thought of all the happy days and years we had lived together, and I was grateful. What if Queenie had decided to stop somewhere other than Uncle's sawmill to rest until her pups were born? I'd never have known him. Such an idea was so absurd I smiled. He'd had to be mine. I was his boy; he was my dog.

About Lonnie Coleman

A native of Georgia, Lonnie Coleman is well known both as a novelist and a playwright. His play *Next of Kin* appeared as the movie "Hot Spell," and his eight novels, among them *Sam, The Golden Vanity,* and *Adams' Way,* have received critical and popular attention. The group of short stories, *Ship's Company,* was highly acclaimed by reviewers. Mr. Coleman has been a member of the editorial staffs of *Collier's, Ladies' Home Journal, Good Housekeeping,* and is at present an editor of *McCall's* magazine.